"I need a—woman-friend for a few days."

Elyss knew that there was more behind it than he was stating. "What's the matter, Pendleton, your charm failing?"

Totally serious, he went on. "In return for you giving me five days of your time, I am prepared to cancel all present and future debts in relation to repairs to your vehicle and mine."

Elyss stared at him dumbstruck. There had to be a catch! "What's the snag—accepting that I'd have to put up with you for five days?" she queried warily.

She saw his mouth move almost imperceptibly, as though she made him want to smile. He didn't smile though. "I said I needed a 'woman-friend,' I didn't mean enemy."

"I can be a friend," she said. "To be free of a debt *that* big, I can be a jolly good friend."

Jessica Steele lives in a friendly English village with her super husband, Peter, and a boisterous, manic but adorable Staffordshire bull terrier dog called Florence. It was Peter who first prompted Jessica to try writing, and after the first rejection, encouraged her to keep on trying. Luckily—with the exception of Uruguay—she has so far managed to research inside all the countries in which she has set her books, traveling to places as far apart as Siberia and Egypt. Her thanks go to Peter for his help and encouragement.

Books by Jessica Steele

Temporary
Girlfriend
Jessica Steele

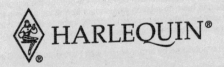

TORONTO • NEW YORK • LONDON
AMSTERDAM • PARIS • SYDNEY • HAMBURG
STOCKHOLM • ATHENS • TOKYO • MILAN • MADRID
PRAGUE • WARSAW • BUDAPEST • AUCKLAND

ISBN 0-373-03525-X

TEMPORARY GIRLFRIEND

First North American Publication 1998.

Copyright © 1997 by Jessica Steele.

This edition published by arrangement with Harlequin Books S.A.

® and TM are trademarks of the publisher. Trademarks indicated with ® are registered in the United States Patent and Trademark Office, the Canadian Trade Marks Office and in other countries.

Printed in U.S.A.

CHAPTER ONE

ELYSS drove into the forecourt of the well maintained block of flats where she lived. A smile touched the corners of her lovely mouth as she parked in her usual place and thought of the contrast between where she had driven from and where she had arrived.

She let herself in through the main door of the building, musing: forget the quiet, forget the serenity of the weekend she had just spent with her parents in their Devon cottage; her forty-eight hours of peace and tranquillity were over.

Not that she minded—now. Up until five months ago, though, she had been living on the outskirts of London with her parents in a household where raised voices were seldom heard. Which was why, when she had started sharing the flat, she had at first been constantly startled by the top-of-the-range squeals that had assaulted her ears as an outraged Victoria would demand of Nikki, 'Have you got my hairdryer?' and Nikki would retaliate at high pitch, 'Have you borrowed my black shoes again?'

Elyss had adjusted—now. But she guessed that her bewilderment, her fear that she might have made the wrong decision when she had answered the 'Fourth wanted to share flat' advertisement must have shown. Because Louise, the eldest of her flatmates and, Elyss was to discover, the more steady of the three, had told her not to worry and that the other two would calm down in a few minutes.

Which was true. In no time at all Victoria and Nikki would forget all hostility and, as suddenly as they had flared up, they were the best of friends again.

Elyss took the stairs to their second-floor flat feeling lucky to be part of the group. The flat was intended to be a three-bedroomed apartment, but when Nikki, who seemed to lurch from crisis to crisis, had lost her job over her poor time-keeping, she could not pay her share of the rent in full.

Louise, Victoria and Nikki had a conference where Victoria confessed that she was struggling financially, and Louise owned to being stretched money-wise on account of her twelve-year-old son. Her ex-husband paid Thomas's boarding school fees, but it seemed that never a month went by when the growing boy wasn't in urgent need of something. It was her ex-husband's view that in paying his son's school fees he was already doing far more than he should—anything extra was down to Louise.

The upshot of the conference was that having a fourth flatmate to pay a share of the rent and service bills would help them all out. What did they need with a separate dining room anyway? It would make an ideal fourth bedroom.

All this Elyss had learned later. At that time her family were having to make tough decisions as her father could ignore no longer that his failing business was past saving. It was time to stop throwing good money after bad.

But that was then, and Elyss did not want to dwell on a time that had been so heart-rending for her family.

She inserted her key into the door of the flat and wondered instead how her flatmates had fared that weekend. By now she was used to the weekly disasters that seemed to befall Nikki, and, though she had blonde hair herself, Elyss reflected that blondes didn't come any dizzier than Nikki.

'Anyone home?' she called as she let herself in.

'Hi!' Louise, a pretty, brown-haired woman who, at thirty-two, was ten years older than Elyss, appeared from the kitchen. 'Had a good weekend?'

'It's always good to see my parents.' Elyss smiled, dropping her weekend bag down for a minute or two. 'Anything happened here?'

'Victoria's out with some new man, and Nikki's still being messed about by Dave.'

'Oh, grief! She was supposed to be going out with him last night. Didn't…?'

'He didn't show. She's gone over to his place now. I know, I know. I've told her if you want a man to chase you, you have to run in the opposite direction—in my case I didn't run fast enough and got caught,' Louise inserted drily, 'but she won't listen. I think it's the real thing this time—with Dave, I mean. I think she's in love with him.'

They fell to commiserating about Nikki; for all that she was the youngest, Elyss, like Victoria and Louise, had soon fallen into feeling protective about her. 'There's nothing we can do to help, I suppose.'

'Short of dropping something unpleasant on Dave's head from a great height, not a thing,' Louise answered. 'Fancy a cup of tea?'

While Louise was making the tea Elyss rang her parents to let them know, as they'd requested, that she had made it to London without mishap. Then she took her weekend bag to her room. She emptied it, feeling for Nikki because she was going through such a bad time over the man she was in love with. Elyss had never been in love herself, or remotely anywhere near it, and with Dave giving Nikki the run-around, she didn't know that she wanted to be.

She and Louise were finishing their tea when Nikki, fretful and unsmiling, arrived home.

'He wasn't in?' Louise enquired gently.

Nikki shook her head. 'I waited around for ages. In the end, what with neighbours' curtains twitching and everything else, I expected the police to arrive any minute in answer to someone's call reporting a stranger casing the area. I decided to catch a bus home—have you ever tried catching the bus you want on a Sunday?'

Elyss had forgotten—Nikki, after another financial crisis, had sold her car. 'Would you like some tea?' Elyss offered sympathetically.

'Ooh, I'd love a cup,' Nikki accepted gratefully, but seemed unable to settle, 'I'll—er—just take the phone to my room and make a call while you're brewing up.'

Elyss went to make a fresh pot of tea, knowing, as did Louise, that by the look of her Nikki was going to try to reach her errant boyfriend by phone.

Elyss returned with three cups and saucers on a tray, noticing as she went into the sitting room that the phone was back on its station. One glance at Nikki's face was sufficient to tell her that Dave must still be out.

'I thought we'd join you,' Elyss said brightly, explaining the extra cups and saucers.

'What a good idea,' Louise remarked cheerfully—but Nikki was not impressed by either girl's brightness or cheerfulness.

'It's no good. I shall have to go over again. I...'

'Nikki!' Louise cried in alarm. 'He's not worth it.'

'I know,' Nikki answered. 'He's a snake, a slug, but I shan't be at rest until I've had it out with him.' And, tea forgotten in her haste to be away, she turned to Elyss, 'I don't suppose, buses being what they are on a Sunday, you'd lend me your car, would you?'

Elyss stared at her, uncertain how to reply. She was unsure if her car insurance allowed Nikki to drive her car—and immediately felt small-minded. Nikki had an unblemished driving licence, and Victoria was always letting her use her car. Victoria would have done so now, Elyss knew, so she guessed there must be some insurance clause that covered the situation.

'Of course,' she smiled, still wanting to help, though she was uncertain if Nikki going to confront her boyfriend would truly help.

Nikki didn't waste any time once she had Elyss's car keys and went hurrying from the flat. 'Tea?' Elyss offered Louise with a sigh, picking up the pot.

'Why not?' Louise grinned.

Elyss spent the evening doing some laundry, watching a half-hour of television and generally chatting to Louise. Victoria came home around eleven, but there was no sign of Nikki when they decided, tomorrow being a work day, it was time for bed.

Somehow, as Elyss saw in her mind's eye Nikki sitting in the car outside Dave's flat waiting for him to come home, she found sleep elusive. Oh, she did so hope Dave returned alone.

Elyss adjusted her position in her comfortable bed. She fleetingly recalled it was her bed from her old home, an elegant Georgian house that was gone now, like her father's business.

She had worked in the company, had done so ever since she had left school. Her father had trained her in administration, and the more she had learned the more she had enjoyed the work she did. Being the boss's daughter, however, had allowed her to be privy to the most confidential matters. Which was all to the good while the wholesale fruit importing business was doing well—but exceedingly worrying when it started to fail.

Elyss had seen the crash coming, and had tentatively broached the subject to her hard-working father. But he had only teased her for being a worrier over nothing. 'It's not unnatural for a company as large as ours to experience the occasional hiccup,' he'd smiled. 'Things will work themselves out, you'll see. Er—meantime, not a word to your mother.'

Her father's obvious confidence had quietened her worries. He had been in this business all his life, for goodness' sake. What did she know!

So she waited, and waited for 'things to work themselves out', only they didn't. And loath though she was to bring the subject up again, after a year had gone by and not only was business not picking up, but they were getting deeper and deeper into debt with the bank, she plucked up courage to question her father if there was anything they could do about it.

'We'll have to try and ride it out,' her father had replied—only there was no confident smile this time.

They had not been able to ride it out. Month after month had gone by as the company had limped along. Their bank manager had tried to help all he could, but it seemed there were limits to his powers.

Elyss would never forget the afternoon when, his face grey, her father had returned from a meeting with the bank manager, and told her that the company was folding.

'Folding!' she'd echoed, leading him to a chair and sitting him down. He'd looked on the point of collapse when for the next half-hour they discussed the ending of what had been life's blood to him.

They'd said nothing to the workforce. Shaken herself, but seeing that her father still didn't look any better, Elyss had insisted on driving him home.

Because he was essentially a very private man, she made herself scarce while he went and revealed the truth to her mother. Elyss knew it would be a most humbling experience for him.

Her mother, though, like the wonderful person she was, was marvellous. Elyss, fretful in her room, was relieved no end to hear her father leave the drawing room and come out into the hall and call, his tone sounding much firmer than it had: 'Come down, Elyss. Your mother—er—and I, want a family conference.'

Her mother had apparently sensed for some while that something was wrong. But when all her approaches to her husband to find out what had been brushed aside as pure imagination, she had started to consider all sorts of possibilities.

Although the news that the business had gone under was a fairly devastating shock, it was a tremendous relief that her husband had neither a mistress, nor some dreadful terminal illness he was trying to hide from her.

'Well, the first essential is to try to see to it that we come out of this with as much honour as we can salvage,' she stated proudly, and they were all agreed on that.

As they agreed about almost everything else to do with winding up the company. The only point on which they had a disagreement was when—their creditors by now baying to be paid—Elyss determined that the money settled on her by her parents on her eighteenth birthday should go into the family kitty.

'Oh, no, I'm not taking that. It's yours, its—'

'It's ours, Dad,' Elyss interrupted him gently. 'The house is going, and anything else of value. I'm part of this family. I shall take it as a personal insult if you don't allow me to contribute.'

He huffed, he puffed, but the pride of not owing his creditors anything finally won. 'You wretched child,' he called her lovingly, 'Come and give your old Dad a kiss.'

So they had settled all their accounts, and were left with nothing over; their only assets were three cars, not new but purchased in better times, and a small amount of jewellery, the value of which was mainly sentimental.

With the house sold and the purchasers wanting completion within six weeks', all that remained was for Elyss and her father to find jobs and somewhere for them all to live.

It was then, after having had so much go wrong in their lives, that their luck began to turn. Quite out of the blue her mother had a letter from a firm of solicitors informing her of an inheritance from a distant relative.

With great excitement they had contacted the legal firm and the next day were in Devon inspecting the two-bedroomed cottage, sorely in need of modernising.

Anne Harvey finished her inspection of her dilapidated inheritance and took a deep breath. Then, as they stood in the wilderness of the large garden looking at the whitewashed walls of the rickety cottage, she calmly announced, 'I should be quite happy to live here.'

Husband and daughter stared at her. But it was her husband who, clearly adoring his wife, commented quietly, 'You always were an optimist, old love.'

Conversation on the drive home consisted almost entirely of the three of them moving to Devon, and of how much the modernisation of the cottage they could carry out themselves. Also, what sort of job prospects did father and daughter have in the Devonshire village, which was miles from anywhere?

They had left their Georgian home very early that morning. They returned to find that the postman had delivered a letter bearing another piece of good news. One of Elyss's father's few remaining premium bonds, which he had held for years and forgotten about, had come up.

The money which the premium bond had yielded was not a vast amount, but enough to ease the strain of these last few months. Although once the general euphoria they had all felt at this piece of good luck had worn off, Elyss's father was all for giving the money to her, to go towards replacing the amount which she had insisted on putting into the kitty.

'No way,' she'd declared firmly. 'You'll need all of that to put the cottage back into—' She broke off, a sudden thought coming to her. The idea of her father going to work for someone else after all his years of being his own boss had seriously worried her. 'Unless... You know, if you were really, really careful, I reckon you could eke that money out and live on it until you're old enough to start drawing your pension. You wouldn't have to get a job and...'

'Elyss is right!' her mother took her up straight away. Clearly she had been experiencing the same worries as her daughter about her husband working for someone else. 'I've got all the clothes I shall ever need, and provided we don't hold any outrageous parties...' she tossed in to lighten the atmosphere. They had never gone in for wild parties, and more than a half dozen people in the cottage would make it overcrowded.

Her husband smiled, and Elyss could see that her father was taken with the idea. He had a good year's work in front of him licking the cottage into shape. 'That would give me a chance to look at the wiring. And the plumbing—and that ceiling that looks as though it might fall down at any time.'

'It would be nice to have you home all day,' Anne Harvey smiled. And, least her husband thought her soft, she added, 'If you were very good, I'd even let you help me with that jungle of a garden!'

It seemed settled, but the next day, while her parents were discussing where Elyss was going to sleep until the ceiling in the bedroom she was to have was fixed, Elyss saw the advert for a fourth person to share a flat.

At first she paid only scant attention to it. But when she began to wonder about her chances of finding a job in Devon—she had very good experience in administration and in assisting in the running of a company, but not a single solitary paper qualification to prove it—she started to realise that she might do better looking for work in London. It would be a wrench leaving her parents, of course. But... It was then that she started to believe in the saying, 'Everything comes in threes'.

For it was luck, pure and simple—the third piece of luck for them as a family—that within the next hour Howard Butler telephoned. He was a fruit and vegetable wholesaler who had dealt with her father for as long as she could remember.

'Good morning, Mr Butler. Did you want to speak with my father?' Elyss enquired.

'Not this time. It's you I want to talk to,' he stated, and went on to tell her how he was having a few office problems and needed somebody who knew what they were doing to come and sort things out. 'I was about to advertise, while at the same time wondering who in the trade I might be able to poach.' Plainly he had no compunction about head-hunting. 'When it suddenly struck me that you—who must know the business inside out—might not yet have started looking for a new job.'

'Um, I haven't, actually,' Elyss said, starting to feel quite excited.

'I couldn't pay as much as your father paid you, but if you'd like to come and...'

'You're suggesting I come for an interview?' She couldn't believe it!

'I shouldn't think there's any need for that. I observed you at work when I visited your father's office. The job's yours if you want it—starting the first of next month.'

Heavens! Elyss did some rapid thinking. It was certain she was going to have to get a job. There was absolutely no way she was going to live off her parents in Devon while she looked around for work. 'Er—may I think about it?' she enquired, feeling she should say yes straight away, but also feeling sensitive as to how her parents were going to take the news that she might not be going to Devon with them.

'Let me know tomorrow,' Howard Butler agreed, and, experiencing a mixture of emotions, Elyss put the phone down and turned round to find both her parents watching her.

'What was that about?' her mother asked promptly.

Elyss looked from one to the other—it still seemed incredible that something like this should just fall into her lap. 'I—er—think I've just been—er—to coin a phrase—head-hunted.' She laughed. It was ridiculous. 'That was Howard Butler. He's just offered me a job!'

Ridiculous or not, everything moved quickly after that. Her parents did not want her to stay behind when they left, but neither did they want to stand in her way. However, they wanted to know where she would live. And it was then that Elyss remembered the advert for a fourth person to share.

'Ring now,' her father suggested.

'The tenants will be out at their places of work,' her mother stated.

But, on the off chance that one of them might work unsociable hours, Elyss rang. Nikki was home and sounded so sweet and friendly that Elyss instantly warmed to her. Elyss arranged to go and look at the flat that evening, when the two other residents would be there.

'How did you get on?' her mother asked the moment she returned.

'You know you were sending to auction the furniture you won't be taking to Devon? Well, can I have some of it?'

That had been over five months ago. She had started work at Howard Butler and Company—and had been quietly appalled at the state of his accounting system. How on earth had he ever been able to muddle through? It was a challenge.

A challenge that kept her very busy as she sorted out accounts unpaid and politely chased up the money, and also paid accounts that Howard Butler's company owed. She was currently employed on setting up a more efficient system and ensuring it was working smoothly.

As Howard Butler had said, he couldn't pay her as much as her father had paid her. And what with paying rent, her share of the flat's outgoings, and running her car, Elyss found it a struggle to last from pay-day to pay-day. It was a comfort to know that Louise, Victoria and Nikki had the same problem.

Where was Nikki? Concern over Nikki's present un-happiness had been niggling away in the background the whole while. Elyss turned over in her bed to check the time on her bedside digital clock. Grief, it was ten past one! Where *was* Nikki?

Elyss tried again to sleep, but found her concern for Nikki getting to her. She wondered if Louise and Victoria were awake too and if, like her, they had started to grow anxious about Nikki—the sometimes timid, sometimes funny, scatterbrained, occasionally downright annoying, bag-of-nerves, childlike but most often ex-tremely likeable Nikki.

With sleep nowhere near, Elyss switched on her bed-side light and sat up. She wondered about getting up and going to make a warm drink. She could make one for Louise and Victoria too.

Grief! She was getting as dizzy-headed as Nikki. Victoria and Louise were probably fast asleep in dream-land. She stood to risk waking the pair of them if she went clattering around in the kitchen.

She was just about to try again to sleep, when, at last she heard Nikki's key in the door. Thank goodness for that. She hoped Dave had been kind to her and that there was some good reason for him standing her up. Nikki just didn't deserve that sort of treatment.

Elyss's hand went to the lamp—but she did not switch it off. For just then, and in a flurry of agitation—clearly she was too agitated to knock first on Elyss's door, which was one of the few 'house' rules—Nikki hurried in.

'I saw a line of light under your door. This won't wait until m-morning!' Nikki blurted out in a rush, tears streaming from her deeply unhappy pale blue eyes.

'Oh, Nikki. Nikki, love,' Elyss cried, hating Dave for

doing this to her. 'Come and sit down.' She waited until the broken-hearted Nikki had seated herself on the edge of her bed, and then gently probed. 'What happened? Was Dave...?'

'I d-didn't see Dave,' Nikki wailed. 'I waited and waited and waited, rang his bell, went and tried to phone him, and then went back and rang his bell again, and waited again. And h-he didn't come home!'

'Oh, Nikki, I'm so sorry,' Elyss tried to soothe.

'S-so am I,' Nikki sobbed. 'I w-was so upset when I drove away from D-Dave's place. I just wasn't thinking and—' She broke off to catch her breath, and with fresh tears spurting, she ended, 'And, oh, I'm s-so sorry—I cr-crashed your car.'

'You cr—?' Elyss didn't take it in for a second. 'You crashed my car?' she checked, somehow unable to believe what she was hearing.

'I'm sorry,' Nikki wept. 'I didn't mean to. It just...'

'I should...' Elyss bit down sharp words. 'Of course you didn't,' she said firmly, swiftly getting herself together. 'You're not hurt?' she checked; first things first! 'You haven't been to hospital or...?'

'No. No. Not a scratch. H-he put me in a taxi and told the taxi driver to bring me here.'

'He?' Elyss questioned, taking it slowly—Nikki could get her wires crossed at the best of times. Now, if Elyss was any judge, Nikki was in shock. She would be as brief as possible and see her into bed.

'The m-man I crashed into,' Nikki answered.

Oh, my... 'You crashed into a man?' she asked faintly, pinning her hopes on the fact that if he'd been able to organise a taxi for Nikki then he must still be in one piece.

'Yes. Well, not him particularly. 'I smacked into the s-side of his car.'

'But he—this man—he, and any of his passengers, he—they—they're all right?'

Nikki nodded on a shuddering sob. 'He was by him-self—he didn't seem hurt. He was a bit short with me to start with actually—called me feather-brained—but then, when he could see I was in a bit of a state, he muttered something that didn't sound very complimentary about my driving. He looked at your c-car and said s-something to the effect that I wouldn't be driving that heap again in a hurry, and sent me home.'

Oh, heck—by the sound of it, her car was a write-off. Elyss looked at Nikki, half a dozen questions rushing to be asked. But then she took in how beat, defeated, Nikki looked. Added to that, Nikki was ashen and shaking. So Elyss reckoned that any further questioning could wait until morning.

She took Nikki to her room and advised, 'Get into bed,' and, unsure what the treatment was for shock, she added gently, 'I'll go and get you a couple of aspirins and a cup of sweet tea.'

'No thanks. I don't want anything. I j-just want to die.'

'Oh, come on, love. It isn't as bad as that,' Elyss said bracingly. 'I'll go and get you a hot water bottle.'

Nikki was in bed when she got back. Elyss handed her the bottle, told her that she mustn't worry about a thing—and left her to go and do some worrying of her own.

Her first concern was Nikki, who she could see was extremely troubled. From what Elyss had just observed, Nikki just wasn't up to anything else going wrong with her world. Another disaster, and it seemed to her that her hare-brained flatmate would be even more emotionally distressed.

Well, Nikki would get no pressure from her. Okay, so Nikki had written off her car. Written off—oh, grief! How was she going to get to work in the morning?

Perhaps Nikki hadn't exactly wrecked it. Perhaps it just looked that way. And why worry about work in the morning? By the sound of it, she was going to have to spend her morning in arranging to get her vehicle towed away from where Nikki had abandoned it, and in making contact with her insurance company.

For the man Nikki had crashed into to be able to tell the taxi driver where to take her meant that Nikki had obviously exchanged names and addresses. Elyss remembered how, only a couple of months ago, she had written a cheque when her car insurance had become due. Nikki would have been able to tell the other driver the name of her insurance company too, Elyss reflected, looking for good points in the whole of this mess. Because by sheer chance Nikki had had a job interview near to the insurance company. 'Save yourself a stamp,' she had chirruped in that sweet way of hers. 'My interview's tomorrow; I'll drop your cheque in as I'm passing.' Nikki had not got the job.

Elyss's thoughts stayed with insurance companies, hoping that she hadn't given herself a problem with hers by allowing Nikki to drive her car. She must check that with Victoria in the morning.

Elyss adjusted her alarm to go off a half-hour earlier in the morning. Perhaps with an early start she might not have to take the whole of the morning off work. She fell asleep pondering. If no one was hurt, was one obliged to report an accident to the police?

Having had less than four hours' sleep, Elyss did not

want to get up when her alarm wakened her. She opened her eyes, remembered—and stifled a groan. Shrugging into her robe, she pattered into the kitchen to find that Nikki was already up.

'Oh, Elyss, I'm so sorry,' she apologised fretfully once more, before Elyss could so much as wish her, Good morning.

Nikki had a little more colour in her face now, Elyss was glad to note, but she still had that anxious, haunted look about her. 'Try not to worry,' Elyss smiled, while trying hard to keep her own worries down. 'The insurance companies will settle both claims, and I can travel by bus until—' She broke off. Nikki had gone ashen again. 'Wh—?'

'Oh, Elyss. I really am so sorry,' Nikki apologised yet again, only this time she put her hand in her dressing gown pocket and handed her an envelope—and started to cry.

'Don't cry...' was as far as Elyss got before glancing down at the envelope; she recognised her own writing. It was the envelope she had addressed to her insurance company a couple of months ago!

A feeling of dread shot through her. Even while part of her brain was denying what Nikki's tears and the sealed envelope might possibly mean, Elyss began to experience panic.

Quickly she slit open the envelope. At speed she took out its contents. Oh, no! It couldn't be! But—it was. There, in her hand, along with her letter and details, was the cheque she had written to the insurance company. 'You didn't...' she choked hoarsely.

'I forgot,' Nikki agonised, her distress quite desperate. 'It was only when—in between worrying about Dave and your poor car, but thinking how your c-car insurance would pay for everything—I suddenly realised that I'd never handed the cheque in. I know it's no excuse, but I put that envelope in a separate compartment in my bag so it wouldn't get all crumpled. Only, as the hours and minutes ticked by and that job interview got nearer and nearer, I got so jittery—that everything else went out of my head.'

'And you didn't think about it afterwards!' Elyss gasped, belatedly realising she had been remiss herself in not following up when no certificate of motor insurance had come through the post. When it hadn't arrived she had just assumed it had gone to her old address by mistake and would catch up with her. She supposed she should blame pressure of work, staying late reorganising, for making her forget all about it. But, oh, grief, she had been happily driving around these past two months without motor insurance. Oh, heavens, she was uninsured!

So much for thinking that there must be some clause in her insurance that allowed Nikki to drive her car. Neither of them was insured. Oh, my sainted aunt, to have moved that car so much as an inch on the highway had been a criminal act!

'Oh, don't be cross with me! Please don't be cross with me, Elyss,' Nikki begged, fresh tears falling. 'Everything's going so terribly wrong for me just now.'

'Oh, Nikki!' Elyss answered helplessly, again aware of how very distracted Nikki was. She was starting to feel much the same way herself as it very quickly dawned on her that there would be no money forthcoming to replace her written-off car. But, worse than that, there would be no money from her insurance company to pay for the repairs to the car which Nikki had crashed into either! Criminal! If she couldn't find the money out of her own pocket, she could be sued in the courts for it!

She pulled herself away from her own worries as she became aware that Nikki was getting herself into something of a state again. 'It's all right!' she tried to soothe. All right? Thanks to Nikki she could end up with a criminal record! Ye gods! It didn't bear thinking about. Yet she just couldn't ignore it and hope that it would go away. 'Sit down, Nikki,' she instructed, and as Nikki complied, dabbing at her eyes, Elyss found it impossible to sit down herself. 'I'll make a pot of tea,' she said as kindly as she was able—and got busy, her mind shooting off at a tangent.

She didn't have any money to pay for repairs! She could end up with a criminal record! Calm down. So, okay, she had been in complete ignorance about the fact that she wasn't insured. She had given her cheque to someone else to pay the insurance for her—oh, that was certain to go down well in court! Heavens—her parents! They'd be thunderstruck that, within months of leaving them, she had landed herself in this mess.

But it wasn't her mess, it was Nikki's. Oh, Lord. Elyss could just imagine Nikki's reaction if she so much as mentioned court. She sighed, realising full well just then that it might be Nikki's mess, but *she* was the one who was going to have to clear it up.

She poured some tea and felt wretched when, as she handed Nikki a cup, she saw that Nikki's hands were shaking so much she could barely hold it.

'Come on, Nikki,' she said bracingly, sounding far more confident than she felt, though her initial shock was starting to wear off. 'Nothing's as bad as that.'

'You reckon!' Plainly Nikki didn't believe it, and Elyss wasn't convinced herself, but nothing was going to be achieved by both of them breaking down in floods of tears.

She tried hard to be objective. Perhaps, as she'd told Nikki, nothing was so bad. Perhaps, if the damage to the other car was only slight, she might be able to settle. If she asked Howard Butler for an advance on her salary—though that would mean letting him know she lived from pay-day to pay-day, of course, and it would bruise her pride. Oh, grief, she couldn't do that! He'd wonder why she couldn't ask her parents for help—and no way was he, or anyone else, going to know that her parents were as hard put to stretch their resources as she was.

'Er—was there very much damage to the other car?' she asked Nikki with seeming casualness, glad to see that, for all her eyes were red and puffy, Nikki had stopped crying.

'I s-sort of caught him semi-sideways on. I think he'll need a new door—at least,' Nikki answered.

Elyss inwardly paled. A new door—that would cost hundreds. 'What sort of car was it?' she followed on, praying for something small: a mini would suit, but even that wouldn't come cheap.

Nikki swallowed. 'A Ferrari, I think.'

A Ferrari! Elyss's legs went weak—forget hundreds, she needed to think thousands. Great! The way her luck was going Nikki had most likely crashed into some judge, or, at the very least, some chief constable. 'You exchanged names?' She sat down—this *was* a nightmare!

Nikki put her hand into her other dressing gown pocket and withdrew a small card which she passed over. Elyss took it. It was a business card. Saul Pendleton was neither a judge nor a top policeman, Elyss saw. She registered the fact that Saul Pendleton worked for a firm

called Oak International. His card gave both his home
and office address, and he had a flat in a *very* plush area
of London. Suddenly she became aware that Nikki was
looking at her as if she had something on her mind.

'What is it?' Elyss asked quietly, having heard enough
to be going on with, and not certain that she wanted to
hear any more.

'I was a bit—er—shaken up last night,' Nikki confessed.

'Yes?' Elyss encouraged.

'I wasn't thinking clearly.'

Elyss didn't like the sound of this. 'I—don't suppose
you were,' she answered apprehensively.

'He—Mr Pendleton, he was a bit—blunt.' Well, she
had banged into his Ferrari! 'He—um—asked my name,
and...'

'And?'

'And...' Nikki swallowed, and then whispered, 'I—
er—gave him y-your name.'

Elyss's jaw dropped. 'As well as your own, you
mean?'

Nikki shook her head. 'I was too terrified to give him
my name. He was—er—sort of—overpowering. I
couldn't think straight. I just told him I was—Elyss
Harvey.'

Elyss was staring at her in stunned silence when
Louise came into the kitchen. She looked from one to
the other, observing one totally astounded expression
and the puffy red eyes on the other occupant. 'What goes
on?' she asked.

'I hardly know where to begin,' Elyss answered—and
Nikki burst into tears. Ten minutes later, and Louise
knew all that there was to know. Elyss concluded by

passing her the card which Nikki had given her. 'Mr Pendleton works at Oak International. I…'

'Saul Pendleton *is* Oak International—or will be at the end of this year when the present chairman retires and he takes over,' Louise interrupted quietly.

'You know him?' Elyss asked.

'Not personally,' she denied. 'But we're in fibre optics too—we're not a multi-million concern like Oak, of course, but we have small dealings with them from time to time.'

Louise worked as a PA in a forward-looking group and, Elyss had already gathered, knew quite a few people of note in the business world. 'You know of him, though?' she pressed. Louise nodded. 'And?'

Louise gave a hasty glance to Nikki. 'He's—er—got a reputation for being a tough operator. Straight, resolute; try to put one over on him at your peril.'

'Oooh!' Nikki squealed, and at her fresh outbreak of tears, Louise took a firm hand.

'You haven't had much sleep, have you?' she sympathised with Nikki. 'Come on, back to bed.'

Between them they got Nikki into bed. 'Don't worry about a thing,' Elyss heard herself say—when she was a seething mass of worry herself. 'Just try and get some rest.'

'Logic tells me we should be tougher with her,' Louise opined when they got back to the kitchen. 'But she sort of gets to you.'

'I know,' Elyss agreed. 'She's in a shocking state.'

'I thought the same myself. I don't think Victoria's going to work today—something to do with a day she's owed, she was saying on Saturday. We'll get her to keep an eye on Nikki. Now, what are you going to do about…?'

'I'll have to get in touch with Mr Pendleton, I suppose,' Elyss answered; like her, Louise appeared to think that Nikki wasn't up to dealing with it. 'Is he really as tough as you say?'

'Believe it!'

Oh, heck—'try to put one over on him at your peril,' Louise had said, and what had Nikki done but given him a false name? 'What else do you know about him?' Elyss asked. Perhaps he was good to his mother and stray animals. Perhaps he hadn't got a mother. 'How old is he?' she asked, following that train of thought.

'Young to be in the position he's in. Still in his thirties, I think—and a bachelor with it.'

'He doesn't like women?' Elyss questioned, seeing any chance of appealing to his chivalrous side going up in smoke.

'On the contrary. While it's said he keeps his work and his private life in two very separate compartments, it seems he's not lacking for female company.'

'Trust him to have a Ferrari,' Elyss commented, knowing she was being unfairly sour, but getting stabbed by darts of panic from time to time.

'He'll be as mad as hell when he knows he'll probably have to pay for the repairs himself,' Louise volunteered.

Elyss wished she hadn't. 'Insult added to injury,' she sighed. 'I'd better phone him.'

'Do it now—it might *not* be as bad as you anticipate,' Louise advised.

Elyss was reluctant. 'It's too early. He might not be up yet.'

'You think he's got where he is by being a lie-a-bed?'

'Point taken. I'll—er—ring him from my room,' Elyss decided. If she was to be verbally slapped down, she'd rather it was private—even if what Saul Pendleton had to say could not be overheard.

'I'd better go and shower, or I'll be late,' Louise commented and went off to the bathroom, while Elyss went to the sitting room to collect the phone.

'Pendleton,' a clear concise voice answered.

'Oh, good morning. I'm sorry to contact you so early, but I thought you might have a busy day ahead.'

'Did you, now?' Cool, polite, waiting.

'My name's Elyss Harvey.' She quickly got herself together. The pause that followed was almost tangible. He was still waiting. If he was clever enough to be in line for the chairmanship of Oak International, then he was clever enough to remember the name Nikki had given him last night, Elyss thought sniffily. 'My car was in collision with yours last night,' she felt obliged to remind him when he still hadn't said anything.

That did bring forth some response, and his reply sounded every bit as tough as Louise had promised, albeit delivered in silky tones. 'I trust you're not ringing to suggest the mess your vehicle made of mine was my fault.'

'I—er—my vehicle wasn't looking too clever either,' she stated stiffly, something in Saul Pendleton's tone needling her.

'True,' he agreed. 'According to the mechanic who came out, it could be a few days before it's drivable again.'

Her heart leapt. Her car wasn't the write-off Nikki had said it was! Elyss busily tried to estimate the cost of repairs while at the same time frantically searching for some tactful way to let him know that she had neither insurance nor money for her own car repairs—let alone his.

Then she found that her tact, for the moment at any rate, would not be needed. Because clearly Saul Pendleton was not a man with a lot of time to spare to be cluttered up with incidentals. 'I've an appointment shortly,' he stated. 'You'd better come and see me to-night.' He was also a man to whom nobody said 'no', apparently. 'I'll see you at eight.'

With that the line went dead and Elyss was left staring at the phone—stunned! It wasn't eight o'clock in the morning yet—and he had an appointment! Whew—that was life in the fast lane, if you pleased!

She didn't know how she felt about having to meet him that night, at his home presumably, but didn't see that she had very much choice. It would be pointless asking Nikki to go with her. Nikki was in pieces now; she'd fold completely if she had to stand in front of that tough-sounding man and, on top of everything else, had to confess that last night she had lied to him when she had given her name as Elyss Harvey.

Elyss sat on her bed deep in thought for some minutes. It would be wrong to go and meet Saul Pendleton and to pretend that she was the one who had crashed into him last night. She knew that. But it seemed to her that whichever one of them had been driving, the outcome was going to be the same. Elyss had never done anything dishonest in her life, but with Nikki feeling so low and, Elyss judged, unable to take much more pressure— might it not be such a bad idea to keep her out of it completely?

CHAPTER TWO

LOUISE was ready to go to her office by the time Elyss had got herself a little together and emerged from her room. 'How did it go?' Louise asked.

'I'm to go to his home tonight,' Elyss answered.

'He didn't wish to discuss it over the phone?'

'He's busy—unfortunately I'm not in a position to say no.'

'I'm afraid so,' Louise commiserated. 'I'm sorry I can't offer to go with you, but...'

'That's all right,' Elyss smiled, aware that Louise was seeing her ex-husband that evening about a financial matter. She realised, too, that Louise seemed, like her, to know that it was out of the question for Nikki to go. 'I'd better get the Yellow Pages out and start ringing round the all-night recovery services. Apparently my vehicle isn't the write-off Nikki thought. Saul Pendleton called a mechanic out.'

'You could ring and ask him which garage,' Louise suggested.

Elyss recalled the no-nonsense tones of Saul Pendleton. Somehow, given that the Ferrari's owner was somewhere fulfilling his appointment, she felt she would much prefer to hunt through the business section of the telephone directory.

First, however, she went and got ready for her day. That done, she again picked up the phone and found, in actual fact, that it took less time than she would have thought to track down the correct garage. Prompt Motor

Services sounded a very efficient company—and expensive. She asked for a rough estimate of how much it would cost to repair her car—and was quoted a figure that made her eyes water.

'Er—could you give me an estimate for just making it mechanically sound, without dealing with the—er—dents.'

'Dents! You'll need a whole new wing—plus. Aren't you claiming on your insurance?'

'I—er—haven't decided yet,' Elyss replied—and felt just as winded by the lesser and very approximate estimate the garage man gave her. Even that figure seemed impossible to find!

But she would have to accept. To have a car was essential, if she was to get to the area where she worked. Also she had promised her father she would go down to Devon in five weeks' time for his birthday. Her father would meet her at the station, if need be, but train fares were not cheap.

'Would you go ahead with just the essential repairs, please?' she requested, and ended the call. Then she rang Howard Butler to tell him that she would be very late in.

Her next assignment was to present herself at an insurance company where she personally saw to it that her vehicle was insured. Of necessity, she took out the cheaper third party insurance in preference to her normal fully comprehensive cover. But at least she was legally insured to drive. It was a pity that for the moment she did not have a vehicle *to* drive. Then she visited Prompt Motor Services—and was horrified at the damage to her car! No wonder Nikki had been in shock. It was a miracle she had got out of it alive!

Elyss was still feeling shaken herself when, by a most

circuitous route, involving changing transport several times, she made her way to her place of employment. At the end of her working day, she took a similarly tortuous route back home again.

She was late getting in, but was pleased to see that Nikki, though still puffy-eyed, seemed a lot calmer. Elyss saw no point in causing her to get into a state again by revealing that she was shortly going to see Mr Saul Pendleton.

Truth to tell, Elyss was feeling in something of a state herself as she hurriedly showered and changed into an elegant dress of deep blue. As rain was pouring down outside, she topped it with her full-length raincoat.

She was certain it must be the wettest May on record, and it was cold with it. She did not want to arrive at Saul Pendleton's house looking like a drowned rat, and left her room seriously considering the expense of a taxi when Victoria chirruped that she was going out herself. 'Want a lift?' she volunteered.

Louise had already told Victoria about her appointment with Saul Pendleton, Elyss discovered, and they discussed the accident and the state Nikki was in on the way.

'If it goes on like this much longer, we're going to have to persuade her to see Dr. Lowe. Perhaps he'll prescribe something to calm her down,' Victoria said. 'I'd like to get my hands on that Dave!' She pulled up at the smart address Elyss had given her. 'How the other half live!' she exclaimed admiringly as Elyss got out. 'Best of luck!'

'Thanks. And thanks, too, for the lift.'

Elyss squared her shoulders and pushed a smart, glass-panelled door open—and discovered she was going nowhere until she had given the uniformed security man behind a desk in the foyer her name and that of the person she was there to see.

She told him she was Elyss Harvey, and she had come to see Mr Saul Pendleton, and waited while he went to the phone and relayed the information. Then he put the phone down to tell her pleasantly, 'Mr Pendleton is expecting you, Miss Harvey. If you'd like to...'

He saw her over to the lift and was already on the way back to his post as the lift doors closed. Saul Pendleton knew she had arrived!

Elyss had eaten very little that day, a fact she was now glad of as her insides churned, and she wished the next fifteen minutes over. The lift stopped. She got out and at once found the door she was looking for.

She swallowed hard, squared her shoulders again and rang the bell. After a short while the door opened and a dark-haired, grey-eyed bachelor in his mid-thirties stood there.

Elyss was blonde-haired and blue-eyed, like Nikki, and it had been dark when that crash had happened. They were about the same height, and both slender. So why, as the grey-eyed man silently studied her, did it not now seem so simple to make it appear that she and Nikki were one and the same person?

'Good evening, Mr Pendleton.' Elyss did her best, realising that she was supposed to know him, while she kept her fingers crossed that he *was* Saul Pendleton—if he wasn't, she had fallen at the first hurdle.

'Miss Harvey,' he replied, with a look of toughness there in his eyes that suggested 'Don't tangle with me unless you're up to it'. 'Come in,' he invited.

She crossed over his threshold and he closed the door. She waited and then followed him from a most elegant hall into his drawing room, which was the last word in

elegance—and she'd thought the apartment she shared
was smart!

'Do you want to take your raincoat off?' he enquired.
She didn't want to stay that long—but suddenly she was
feeling hot.

'Thank you,' she said, and shrugged out of her coat,
handing it to him. He draped it over a nearby chair.

'Take a seat,' he suggested when she stood in the
middle of his plush carpet wishing she could remember
just one sentence from any of the dozen or so she had
been rehearsing for most of the day.

'Thank you,' she murmured again.

'How did you get here—by taxi?' he enquired as she
settled herself on one sofa and he did likewise on one
opposite.

'A friend gave me a lift.'

'Boyfriend?' he enquired, but she could tell from the
stern look of him that he wasn't particularly interested
in her answer.

'No,' she replied, and left it at that. She could see no
reason to waste further time. 'I'm very sorry about the
accident,' she began for starters.

He observed her silently for a few moments. Then
coolly remarked, 'It's something that you admit liability,
I suppose.'

Oh, heck—was she not supposed to do that? Not that
it mattered; Nikki had said that it was all her fault. Elyss
hesitated. The state Nikki was in, perhaps she'd got it a
little wrong.

'Are you saying that you're a little to blame?' Elyss
enquired hopefully. Even if she had to pay only half it
would be a tremendous relief.

'I'm not saying anything of the sort!' Saul Pendleton
replied sharply. 'As well you know—if you remember

that right turn I endeavoured to make at the traffic lights last night.'

So much for tremendous relief, Elyss mused unhappily, not liking to have her head bitten off for her trouble. Though she took heart that, by the sound of it, he believed that she was the blonde who had crashed into him.

'Who could forget a thing like that?' she murmured. For some unknown reason she was feeling in need of an excuse. 'You know how it is; when the lights changed to green, all I could think of was getting over them before they went to red again. Er—you weren't hurt?' she thought to enquire of this man who was fully in charge and didn't appear to have a thing wrong with him.

'I fared better than my car,' he answered drily.

'I'm sorry about that,' Elyss said. 'About your car, I mean.' And, getting a bit fed up with having to continually apologise—especially for something which she had not done—she enquired politely, 'Have you been able to get an estimate for repairs?' At last they were getting down to the nub of the whole issue.

'Not yet,' he replied, his eyes on her richly blue ones. 'Though, as you'd expect, it will be in the region of at least two thousand pounds.'

Oh, no! Elyss wasn't sure that she didn't lose some of her colour. 'As much as two?' she asked faintly.

'A minimum of two thousand, I'd say,' he replied confidently.

The words trembled on her lips to ask him to get it done somewhere cheaper, but she realised from his clothes, his home, the very manner of him, that he never had anything done on the cheap. 'When is it likely to be finished—repaired?' she made herself enquire. With luck it would take all of a year to get the spare parts.

'The car has been transferred to a specialised garage today. But it will depend on whether parts are available here or whether the garage will have to send to Italy for them. Then they'll be fitting, painting—sorting out the electronics...'

Oh, heck, it *was*, she saw, going to cost all of two thousand pounds. By the sound of it, though, it could take quite a while—but nowhere near long enough for her to be able to scrape the money together.

'Meanwhile, I've been able to hire a car until—'

'You've hired a car?' she cut in in a rush, a note of strain in her voice. This was something she just hadn't thought of. Oh, her stars! The cost of hiring a car would be down to her—she just knew it! She prayed he had hired a small, everyday run-about. But, even as she asked, 'Er—a Ferrari, I suppose?' she knew the answer.

'You suppose correctly, Miss Harvey.'

She started to feel light-headed. Her mind just would not cope with how much it must cost to hire a Ferrari— *and* the length of time Saul Pendleton was going to need to keep it.

She fought to pull herself together and to hide that she was in panic mode. 'The th-thing is,' she began stiltedly. She was here now; there was no point in going away and worrying herself silly. She must try to get something said, sorted out, and settled here and now.

'Yes?' he enquired politely when she had got no further.

At that point Elyss started to actively dislike this man. She had a feeling that he knew she was in one very big mess—but was he saying one word to try and help? Was he, blazes!

She swallowed hard. Be fair. He had been driving along minding his business before her car had side-

swiped him. 'The thing is,' she got started again. 'I
was—er—wondering if you would—um—consider—'
She broke off. He must have the central heating on—
she was all of a lather. 'Consider giving me time to pay.'
Hells bells, at thirty pounds a month—the very maxi-
mum she could scrape together—it would take seven
years *plus* to reimburse him.

He smiled. She liked his smile. It made her feel better.
It seemed he might be prepared to consider her request
anyhow. She smiled back. His dark eyes went from her
blue eyes down to her gently curving mouth.

Then his eyes were back to holding hers, when he
remarked pleasantly, 'Oh, there's no need for that, Miss
Harvey.' Her smile widened—he must have come up
with some answer. She was still smiling when, smoothly,
he added, 'Your insurance company will settle everything, I'm sure.' Abruptly her smile faded, and she
started to dislike him again. 'You *are* insured?' he enquired silkily.

Elyss knew then that he knew that she was *not* insured. She didn't know how he knew, she just instinctively felt it. The knowledge that he was just playing
with her rattled her. 'You know damn well I'm not!' she
flew. She instantly wanted those words back. Oh, grief,
this man missed not a thing. His eyes were on her, taking
in, reading. She lowered her gaze to her lap. 'I thought
I was,' she felt compelled to confess, her tone quieter,
not angry. 'I gave—' She broke off, took a shaky breath
and raised her head to look at him once more. She found
his eyes were still steady on her. He was waiting. From
where she was sitting Elyss realised that she couldn't get
into any more trouble, having owned up to not being
insured. 'A friend was going to drop my cheque into my
insurance company a couple of months ago—only she—

forgot.' Oh, dammit, that sounded so unlikely she was sure he wouldn't believe her.

'You should have checked!' Saul Pendleton stated curtly—and that annoyed her. She knew she should have checked! She didn't need him to remind her.

'*You* obviously did!' she snapped—and got a very grim, unsmiling look for her trouble.

'You think I shouldn't have? After your phone call this morning...' He let that go to change tack, to abruptly question, 'This friend—the one who forgot to drop your cheque off—is she the same friend who was driving your car last night?'

It was unexpected. 'You know?' she gasped. 'You know it wasn't me?'

'Of course I know!' he rapped. 'The woman I spoke with on the phone this morning sounded nothing like the hysterical female I had to deal with last night.'

'She could have calmed down by this morning,' Elyss argued, even though she realised she might fare better if she were placatory rather than argumentative. Yet she didn't seem able to act in a way in which she did not feel. This man, she realised, effortlessly rattled her normally even temperament.

'Not to that extent, she couldn't,' Saul Pendleton gritted concisely. He was right, of course. Nikki had still been in a state this morning. 'Though she might well have remembered that neither car was anywhere near a set of traffic lights when she attempted to demolish my car.'

Elyss gasped in astonishment. Talk about 'Walk into my parlour'! Not minutes ago she had agreed their vehicles had been in collision at some traffic lights!

'You tricked me!'' she exploded angrily.

'Don't get on your high horse that *I* tricked *you*!' he

rapped. 'No one does me down, Miss Harvey! From the way I was hearing it, you were out to have a damned good try.'

She hadn't a leg to stand on. It hurt to back down, but... She drew a shaky breath. 'It wasn't like...' she halted. To tell him how it really was she would have to tell him all about Nikki, and she wasn't ready to do that. 'So—er—after my phone call, you checked with the insurance company. Nikki—' She broke off. She hadn't been going to mention Nikki's name! 'And they told you I wasn't insured.'

'Not with them you weren't. Nor did they know you at the address I was given. You do live there?' he demanded.

'I moved in five months ago—I forgot to give the insurers my change of address.'

She received a grunt for her oversight. There was no point in her explaining that she'd been so busy at work she hadn't had time to think much about anything else— much less to remember to tell people she dealt with only once a year that she had moved.

'You forgot a lot of things by the sound of it.' I wish I could forget you! she thought. The gloves, it seemed, were off. 'You *are* Elyss Harvey?' he questioned toughly. 'Should I decide to sue, will I be confronted by yet another blonde-haired, blue-eyed Elyss Harvey in court?'

Court! Oh, heavens, her parents would be most perturbed. Why couldn't he drive a Metro? 'My name *is* Elyss Harvey,' she confirmed unhappily.

'And your friend?'

'Her name isn't important,' Elyss told him quickly.

'Not important!' He seemed astounded. 'Driving without due care and attention, giving a false name, to itemise but two misdemeanours. We haven't come yet to the criminal act of driving while not insured. Add—'

'She's not well,' Elyss interrupted quickly, having heard quite enough to be going on with. 'She's having boyfriend trouble. She's...'

'She's in a whole heap of trouble!' Saul pronounced curtly. 'And so, if you'll forgive me for saying so, are you.'

Elyss stared at him. This interview wasn't going anywhere near as well as she had hoped. 'Will you not give me time to pay what I'll owe you?' She repeated the question she had asked earlier. The impossible question.

'You work?' he asked bluntly.

'Yes.'

'What do you do?'

'I work, mainly in administration, in a wholesalers.'

'Who?'

She did not like his questions. She did not want to tell him who she worked for. But, she realised, she didn't have a choice. 'Howard Butler and Company,' she reluctantly answered.

'How much do you make?' Cheeky devil! It was none of his business! Though... She stopped short. Of course it was his business. If he was considering allowing her to settle her debt by instalments—which meant he would have to pay the garage bill out of his own pocket—then she supposed he had every right to assess whether she was likely to default on those payments. She told him how much she earned. She hadn't expected him to be impressed. He wasn't.

'I've only been there a short while,' she defended. 'And Mr Butler was so kind in offering me the job, I don't like to ask for more.'

His look said, More fool you, but he refrained from

making such a comment. He enquired instead, 'Is that your sole income?'

She felt embarrassed. Saul Pendleton was quick. He'd have worked out by now that she'd still be in his debt years from now. 'Yes,' she mumbled.

'You live in a smart area,' he stated. 'Pay rent?'

Heavens above! Louise hadn't been joking when she'd said he was a tough operator. Straight, resolute—and you *did* try to put one over on him **at** your peril! Elyss gave a shaky sigh. 'Yes,' she replied. She should never have come. Though what other way was there open to her? 'But there are four of us,' she added. 'We each contribute a—'

'All women?' he cut in abruptly. What had that got to do with anything?

'Of course!' Elyss answered, a shade primly she had to own—but his tone nettled her.

'And how long, even assuming I'm prepared to condone your criminal act,' he inserted, 'do you think you'll be in my debt?'

He knew the answer to that as well as she. She gave him a defeated look. 'What are you going to do?' she asked.

'What do you think I should do?' he tossed back, but did not wait for her to reply. He concisely stripped the whole issue down to one sentence. 'You're criminally uninsured and are ultimately responsible for damage to my vehicle to the tune of at least two thousand pounds. You're not seriously suggesting, the criminal aspect apart, that I do nothing?'

She must have been in cloud-cuckoo-land to have ever accepted his invitation to come here tonight, Elyss realised. 'I suppose not,' she mumbled unhappily, aware that she had achieved nothing other than to discover that she was, financially, in far deeper trouble than she had estimated. That thought panicked her again. 'I don't suppose you could claim off your insurance company, could you?' she asked in a rush.

Saul Pendleton studied her eager expression silently for a moment. Hope grew—and was knocked flat again when he replied, 'I could. But, since I'd have to give them full details of the accident, I'm fairly certain they'd take you to court for the recovery of their money.' Oh, Lord. She was in a mess whatever he chose to do. If he didn't prosecute her then his insurance company would. He stood up, reaching for her raincoat. The interview, it was plain—with no conclusion reached—was over. 'Leave it with me,' Saul Pendleton decreed, holding her raincoat out for her to put it on. 'I'll think about it, and be in touch.'

Her spirits lifted. She turned, buttoning her coat, looking at him. Was there a chance? 'Thank you,' she said quietly, afraid to say more, afraid that he might change his mind, and that any small hope that they could come to some sort of an agreement would be gone. She turned towards the door, and he went with her into the hall. 'You have my address?' she thought to enquire, and wished she hadn't. He'd think her stupid. Of course he had her address—he had commented on it being in a smart area. 'Oh!' she suddenly exclaimed as they reached the hall door.

'Oh?' he queried as she stopped dead and looked up at him.

'C-could I ask you not to call at the flat?' she asked anxiously, in no position to ask favours but...

'I doubt I was proposing to do that,' Saul Pendleton drawled. How was it that she could feel ready to beg while, at the same time, she also felt sorely inclined to stamp her foot down hard on his? He confused her; there was just something about him that affected her oddly. 'But,' he resumed, 'if you'd rather I didn't.'

Sarcastic swine. 'Nikki.' She didn't want to explain— but who held all the aces? Certainly not her. 'She's— er—not coping very well at the moment,' she elaborated. 'She's a bundle of nerves. It would take little more to…'

'Hmm,' he butted in, and did nothing to raise himself in Elyss' popularity stakes when he grunted, 'In which case you should never have let her have your car!' This was a lecture she didn't need! He opened the door and walked her to the lift. 'I'll contact you when I've given your problem some thought,' he pronounced. And that was that.

Elyss made her way back to the flat in a disconsolate frame of mind. Saul Pendleton was treating the matter as her problem rather than his. Which, since he wasn't the one with the threat of court action hanging over him, it was, she supposed dejectedly. But, given that he'd said he would give her problem some thought, the nearer she got to her flat, the more she realised that, as clever as he was, he would not be able to come up with any solution. Nikki might have been the one who crashed into him, but it was her car, and it was she, Elyss Harvey, who hadn't had that car covered by insurance.

The rest of the week dragged by, with Elyss camped near the telephone every evening, ready to snatch it up should it ring. It rang on Tuesday for Victoria, on Wednesday for Louise and on Thursday Elyss's mother telephoned for a chat.

'Everything all right?' her mother asked.

'Couldn't be better,' Elyss replied—there were just some things you didn't worry your parents with.

On Friday evening she and Louise went with Nikki

who had a doctor's appointment. Dr Lowe had been her GP for years, and Nikki was in his surgery for some while. She seemed a little better for having a chat with him, and was keen to start taking the medication he had prescribed.

The weekend dragged by, with Victoria out most of the time and either Elyss and Nikki, or Louise and Nikki, or sometimes all three of them, walking and talking together.

Elyss rang her parents on Sunday, but that was the only time she touched the telephone that weekend. It rang, but the calls were never for her.

She went to work on Monday morning realising that she was going to have to get an additional job. She couldn't do evening work because she never knew how late she was going to have to work at the office. But, except once every five or six weeks, when she travelled down to Devon, her weekends were free.

She had been at her desk for an hour, getting deep into some work and putting to the back of her mind her plans to hopefully find work as a barmaid, a cleaner, a chauffeuse—she was ready to do anything—when the phone on her desk rang.

'You're through,' she heard Peggy the switchboard operator say—then there was silence.

'Hello?' Elyss enquired.

'Pendleton,' replied the voice she had been hearing in her sleep.

She was shaken. She had been waiting for his call. For a week she had been waiting for his call. But not for a moment had she thought he would ring her at her place of work! It threw her. 'What are you ringing me here for?' she asked without thinking.

'You'd prefer that I didn't?' he enquired silkily.

She took a steadying breath. Circumstances decreed that she swallowed her ire. 'No, no,' she denied. 'It's just that I rather supposed you'd ring me at home when you'd—er—er—come to...' Her voice petered out as her throat went dry. He must have decided what he was going to do!

'I had an idea your flat was out of bounds,' he drawled.

'You've—um—got a point there,' she agreed evenly, though he wasn't to know that if Nikki was about, then, the moment Elyss knew it was Saul Pendleton calling, she had planned to take the phone to her room and have her conversation with him in private. Louise and Victoria, however, were acquainted with the fact that she was awaiting this particular phone call. 'You've—er...' Oh, what on earth was she hesitating about? There could be only one reason why he had phoned. 'You've reached a decision?' she asked, and clutched hard onto the phone receiver as she waited to hear what was to be her fate.

She was no further forward after—being nowhere near as shy as she was when it came to blunt talking—he abruptly told her, 'I don't intend to discuss it over the phone. We'll have dinner tonight.'

Oh, will we? Oh, what a man he was for rattling her! Just like that: 'We'll have dinner', and he expected her to jump at the chance! She was about to tell him that she was very fussy about whom she deigned to dine with—why should he think he'd cornered the market on blunt talking?—when it very quickly dawned on her that he was right. If he said jump, then she jolly well had to jump.

'Very well,' she accepted politely, as any well brought up young lady might.

'I gather you'd rather I didn't come to your flat to

collect you?' Clearly he had never doubted but that she would accept.

'You gather correctly,' she replied evenly.

'I'll send a taxi. Be ready at eight.'

He was gone. End of conversation. 'Be ready'—end of story, no debate. What was it about this man that made her go from controlled to confused, from hot and anxious to cross and ready to stamp on his foot? Never had she met a man who could so easily raise her hackles. But then, she wasn't used to being bossed around—it was hard to take. However, she faced it: she was just not in any position to do anything about it.

Elyss made a point of leaving work on time that night. All three of her flatmates were home when she arrived. Nikki was looking a little better than she had last Monday, Elyss was glad to note.

'Do you want to share in the Spanish omelette and salad I'm conjuring up?' Victoria asked cheerfully.

Her Spanish omelettes were most adventurous, Elyss had discovered, consisting mainly of anything left over and cooked inside beaten eggs. 'Thanks, but no. I'm—er—having dinner out tonight,' Elyss declined, and knew she had gone red when three pairs of eyes stared at her.

'You're blushing!' Victoria teased. 'You've got a date! You've actually accepted...'

'Leave her alone, Victoria, there's a love.' This came quietly from Louise.

Elyss looked over to her. Louise was clearer thinking than either Victoria or Nikki. Elyss was fairly certain that Louise had twigged that for 'date' she should read 'second interview with Saul Pendleton'.

'Anyone want a cup of tea?' Elyss asked, her 'date' not up for discussion.

'I'll make it,' Victoria volunteered sunnily. 'You go

and shower and make yourself stunning for Mr
Mystery.'

Elyss had to smile. But she was not smiling when she
stood under the shower. Was she so choosy that Victoria
thought it cause for comment that she'd actually accepted a date with somebody?

Elyss didn't think so. Not that she *was* particularly
choosy—why did she feel she had to defend herself?—
it was just that with work occupying so much of her
time... She had gone out for a meal with one of the men
from work only the other month, she recalled. True, she
hadn't gone out with him again, but that wasn't because
she was too busy; it was simply because she'd found
that one experience so extremely boring!

She'd dated other men before that and hadn't found
it such a dull experience. And she'd kissed quite a few
times too, and found that event enjoyable. Though nothing more than that. Oh, there had been occasions when
her date had wanted to take it further. But she seemed
to have an inbuilt alarm system, and whenever she read
'bed' in any man's eyes, her 'Not tonight, Joe' system
activated itself.

She wasn't frigid, she knew she wasn't. It was just
that her parents had impressed on her, right back in her
early teens, that she was an individual in her own right,
that she had a mind that was completely her own. That
being so, it didn't matter if everyone else in her class at
school had opted to do something or other; unless she
personally felt it was right for her, then she should say
no.

She had never found her individuality a problem.
When she was seventeen, a boy she'd really liked had
wanted her to experiment. She had decided 'no' and,
when he had persisted, she'd decided that she didn't like

him as much as she'd thought she did, and had most definitely said no to him.

Elyss joined her flatmates for a quick cup of tea, reflecting that, though she had dated sufficiently to be quite comfortable in a man's company, none of the men she had known so far had that vital spark.

Why she should suddenly think of Saul Pendleton at the same time as the vital spark was beyond her. He had a certain something, she'd give him that, but he wasn't her type.

In all honesty, she couldn't have said what her type was. But it certainly wasn't some bossy brute who rang and declared, 'We'll have dinner tonight,' and then commanded, 'Be ready at eight.'

CHAPTER THREE

THE taxi arrived a few minutes before eight. Elyss got into it with no idea of where she was heading. All she knew was that she was feeling decidedly jittery. She felt that she was looking good, and she needed every scrap of that confidence. She had a good supply of clothes, and after some silent debate had elected to wear a favourite subdued purple sleeveless silk dress.

The weather had turned warmer at last, or was it knowing she would shortly see Saul Pendleton again, her anxiety, that was causing her blood to rush around? Who wouldn't feel all hot and bothered? It wasn't very pleasant having the Sword of Damocles hanging over one. Whatever Saul Pendleton had decided would mean that she either ended up with a criminal record or she didn't. It was all up to him.

Elyss was feeling more anxious than ever when the taxi slowed to a halt outside a smart hotel. This must be it—where she got out. An attentive hotel doorman had the taxi door open before she could blink. She stood on the pavement about to settle with the driver when Saul Pendleton appeared in front of her. The taxi pulled away, and she realised the driver must have already been paid.

She looked up at her host. He was as tall as she remembered him. She felt oddly tongue-tied as her eyes met his. Ridiculous. 'Good evening, Mr Pendleton,' she greeted him crisply.

She observed that there was a hint of a smile on his mouth—it was actually a very nice mouth—as he studied her a moment longer. But that smile did not quite make it. 'Saul,' he suggested and, placing a hand beneath her elbow, he escorted her into the hotel.

Her hopes lifted. Would he invite her to call him by his first name if he had something not very nice to tell her? Hope dipped. He probably would. He was smooth, sophisticated.

They were seated in a lounge area and soon making their selections from a leather-bound menu, but Elyss was barely able to concentrate. The condemned man ate a hearty meal, or, in this case, woman. She put down her menu. 'Have you come to a decision?' she questioned abruptly.

Slowly Saul Pendleton lowered his own menu, his expression inscrutable. 'I thought I might try the halibut,' he replied pleasantly.

She wanted to hit him. 'I didn't mean about what to eat. I meant have you decided about...'

'Shh,' he hushed her. 'Let's not ruin our digestion.'

'As bad as that?' she questioned, realising that, by the sound of it, whatever decision he had come to it was going to be unpalatable.

He smiled, almost as if she had amused him. Oddly, her heart seemed to miss a beat. This was absurd, she didn't want to amuse him. She wasn't here to entertain him, for goodness' sake!

But, since it seemed that he was in no hurry to have a discussion about the reason for their meeting, Elyss felt forced to put her anxieties on hold and proceed with dinner.

By coincidence, she also chose fish for her main course, fish in a mushroom sauce. And, strangely in her view, once they were seated at their table and tucking into the first course, she discovered Saul Pendleton was a very agreeable host. He appeared able to converse on any subject, and, unlike the man from her work place whom she had dined with, he was never dull.

What was more, even while she knew that she didn't have half of his knowledge, he neither talked down to her, nor in any way gave her the feeling that he thought her answers lightweight. 'You have a lively mind,' he even commented at one stage. So she felt heartened that perhaps he didn't think her boring either.

They were well into their main courses when he asked her about her job. 'You're young to have a job as an administrator,' he remarked, when she told him a little about her work.

'I'm twenty-two,' she replied, 'and I cut my teeth on office administration.' She decided she did not want to tell him any more, but she had reckoned without him wanting to know more.

'You're not going to leave it there?' he teased.

And for no reason—she wasn't even sure if she liked him—Elyss had to smile, and found she was going on, 'My father trained me—he had his own business. I joined the firm as soon as I was old enough.'

'You said "had". Your father had his own business.' Grief, was he sharp on the uptake!

'We—er—hit a sticky patch...'

'About five months ago?'

Had she said sharp? Razor-edged, more like! 'Close,' she conceded. 'Though the sticky patch turned out to be more like quicksand.'

'You—your firm—it folded?'

'Sank without trace,' she had to agree. However, her pride was out in full force when she added, 'We paid all our debts. Nobody else went to the wall because of us. We—my father—sold everything, including our home in Berkshire, rather than go bankrupt.'

A waiter appeared. Without her being fully aware of it they had finished their main course. Their plates were taken away, and Saul suggested a ten-minute respite before they ordered their last course.

'So you see,' Elyss took up again, only then realising that she had an opening here, 'it was the foulest blow—er—in more ways than one—when Nikki pranged into your car.'

'You honestly had given her a cheque to pay your car insurance?'

'Don't you believe me?' It annoyed her that her honesty was being questioned, her indignation causing her to forget she had been on the way to underlining the difficulty she would have in finding the two thousand pounds plus required all at once. She stared hostilely into Saul's face—and wondered what in creation was going on in her heart when he started to smile and it seemed to skip yet another beat.

'Do you know?' he drawled. 'I rather think I do.'

Elyss looked away from him and down, finding the tablecloth of much interest. 'Well, anyway, the cheque and details were in an envelope which Nikki volunteered to drop in for me on her way to a job interview...'

'But when it came to it, she forgot because of her nervousness about what was in front her?'

'Do you sleep in the knife-box?' Elyss looked at him to question. Sharp! Razor-sharp! Amend that to laser.

'Elementary, my dear Elyss,' he misquoted, and she felt decidedly shaky. 'Is your car insured now, by the way?' he thought to enquire.

'It has been since last Monday. Though it's still not repaired yet.'

'You've been able to give instructions for the repairs to be carried out?'

That was one tactful way of asking if she could afford it! 'The dents will take a little longer, but they've said they'll make it mechanically sound. It will make getting to work a whole lot easier,' she felt she should explain. 'And I need it when I go to Devon to see my parents. I'm going to look for weekend work.' She thought she should mention that, in case he thought she wasn't making any effort to get the money together in order to eventually settle her debt to him.

He barely seemed to notice, but questioned instead,' Your parents moved to Devon?'

'They say the darkest hour is just before the dawn,' she commented. 'Everything had gone, when suddenly our luck changed.' Well, her parents' luck had; in view of her car enthusiastically kissing his Ferrari, she was having second thoughts about her own.

The waiter returned and they both ordered cheese and biscuits to finish with; a selection was brought to them in no time.

'Tell me about this change of fortunes,' Saul prompted.

'An—' She broke off. He looked at her, took his time over her deeply blue eyes, her dainty nose and lovely mouth, his gaze straying to her straight blonde hair that just turned under a couple of inches before it might reach her shoulders. 'I've done nothing but talk about me and my family all evening,' she protested.

'Quite untrue,' he stated, his grey eyes back on her stunning blue ones again. 'But,' he shrugged, 'if you don't want to talk about you or your family, tell me about your man-friend.'

'There isn't one!' she retorted.

'You sound upset about it.'

'Oh, for g—' she began to explode, and then realised from the devil lurking in the grey depths of his eyes that he was baiting her. 'My mother was left a cottage in Devon by a long-lost aunt,' she swiftly changed course. She was amazed when, at her abrupt departure from the subject at hand, he burst out laughing.

She had to laugh herself. My goodness, what an evening! She didn't know how he'd done it, but she had been so jittery and so hot and bothered on the way here, and now Saul Pendleton had somehow made her so relaxed, feel so at ease, she was actually laughing with him!

She sobered. There were still very important matters to be discussed here. Saul hadn't wanted to talk about his decision before dinner, but their meal was virtually over.

She opened her mouth, thinking she was about to ask him what his decision was, and heard her voice enquire, 'So in which dark cupboard do you keep your family? You don't seem to want to talk about them.'

'There's no dark cupboard,' he replied easily. 'My parents live in Hertfordshire. I've a sister who lives in Warwickshire. I don't have a wife,' he tacked on.

'I know,' Elyss said without thinking, and felt herself go pink in case he thought she had been checking up on him. 'A-about you being a bachelor, I mean. Louise, one of the women I share with, the firm she works for has—' She broke off, fearing she might be doing Louise a disservice. 'I'd—er—never heard of you,' she felt bound to go on, starting to feel hot again. 'But when I showed Louise the card you'd given Nikki, she said she had. Heard of you, I mean.' Grief, she was rambling! Firmly, she closed her lips.

'So you don't have a particular man-friend. You like to play the field?'

Elyss stared at him, wishing she could swap and hop onto his wavelength as easily as he did hers.

'I don't have time to—' She broke off. According to her mother you could *find* time for anything you *truly* wanted to do. 'That is, I don't date just anyone. Oh, grief. That sounds as if I'm unbearably fussy. I'm not, it's just—' She broke off again, could feel herself growing warm again. 'It's not that I'm frigid.' Had she just said that? 'Look, can we change the subject?' How had she got herself into this? He was either going to think her a nut or a nymphomaniac!

'It embarrasses you to talk about sex?' he enquired easily, all too obviously having no problem with it himself.

'It's not something I do normally,' she answered a degree more coolly, but he was not put off.

Though he paused for a moment, and leaned back in his chair to study her speculatively. It did not help her feeling of being hot under the collar. 'Talk or act,' he enquired pleasantly. 'Which do you not normally do?'

'I meant talk,' she replied coldly.

Saul Pendleton stared at her for a few studied moments, and then replied, 'But I think both apply.'

He annoyed her. Even though she was fully aware that she could not afford the luxury of letting herself be so, he annoyed her all the same. From the little she had said it seemed he suspected, accurately as it happened, that she had never been to bed with a man. She had no intention whatsoever of confirming it for him.

'You may think what you please,' she made herself reply pleasantly. Bigger things were at issue here. Dinner was over. 'May I now know—?' A waiter hovering

caused her to break off, and what she wanted to know
had to wait while he served them with coffee and petit
fours. Once he had gone away again, she was about to
again politely enquire what decision Saul Pendleton had
come to, but did not get the chance.

'I've been invited to a party this coming Saturday.'
He spoke first, throwing her completely. Now what tack
was he on?

'A-Are you going?' She wanted to talk motor repairs
and the non-payment thereof—he wanted to talk *parties*!

'I want you to come with me.'

Elyss stared at him in amazement, struggling to com-
prehend what this had got to do with anything. Then
wondered shakenly—did it? Did it have something to do
with the car accident? 'Given that I'm in your debt...'
Colossally in his debt, if she were not to make too fine
a point of it! 'Why me?' she asked bluntly. He didn't
fancy her, she knew that. His taste would run to a much
more sophisticated type of woman.

'Why not you? You said not long ago you were looking for weekend work.'

'You didn't know that when you told me we'd have
dinner tonight.' This had never been an invitation! 'And
you could have told me about this party over the phone,'
she added for good measure. She didn't want to go to
any party with him, and felt nettled that she was being
backed into a corner, where she would find it difficult
to refuse him.

He was unperturbed by her hostility. To her annoyance she would swear that the corners of his mouth even
twitched as he commented, 'You're an argumentative
little lady. However, it was only this morning I decided
but, since phoning you at home wasn't possible, and
since you and I both have busy working lives, it seemed

better to discuss any objection you might have over dinner.'

She could swallow that—just. 'This sounds an important kind of party?' she questioned.

'Roland Scott—the present chairman of Oak International, and a man I have a great respect for—is celebrating his wedding anniversary. He and his wife have decided to mark the event with a party.'

The party would be very pleasant, she was sure, but that still did not explain—why her? To hear Louise tell it, he knew women by the score. If he wanted some female on his arm, why not take one of them. 'You want to take me in order to make some woman also going to the party jealous?' She worked out the best logical answer she could find.

'Hardly,' he replied.

She wasn't sure how she felt about that. He either meant 'hardly' because that wouldn't be his style, or 'hardly' because no woman he was that keen on would be jealous of her. 'So why ask me, then, and not one of your lady-friends?' she asked shortly. 'According to Louise you've got them by the dozen.'

'She flatters me,' he commented smoothly.

Which to her mind was no sort of an answer. She gave an exasperated sigh. She didn't want to go to any party but, if she had to, she needed to know more than he seemed willing to tell her. 'So where do I come in, then?' she asked bluntly, still trying to sort through the very little she knew to find an answer for herself. 'You don't want to make some female jealous, yet you know I'm going to have to agree to go with you, whether I want to or not.'

He shrugged. 'Who said you had to enjoy it?'

'I've sinned—this is my punishment?'

'Do you always view an evening's entertainment in this manner?' he asked off-handedly.

'Not when I have the option of turning down those offers that don't appeal,' she retaliated, objecting to him making her sound like a killjoy. Normally she enjoyed parties. Straightforward parties. But there was more in this than Saul Pendleton was saying; she just knew it. 'So this is to be my way of settling my debt,' she documented, still searching. 'Well, part payment,' she quickly amended when his right eyebrow went aloft.

'You were the one who spoke of finding weekend work,' he reminded her.

Heaven knew how many weekends she'd have to work to pay back the kind of money in question. But suddenly all her nerve-ends started to jangle. He'd seemed as comfortable talking of sex as he might have been talking about the weather. Was he expecting her to go to bed with him at the end of Saturday evening? 'You don't...' she began in alarm.

'I don't?' he queried, for once not on her wavelength.

'You—haven't any plans to... Afterwards, after the party...' she questioned chokily—and found that his inability to follow her thought pattern had only been temporary.

'What—and get frostbite?' he tossed at her—for all she had told him that she wasn't frigid.

She felt she should apologise, but did not want to. Instead, since he wasn't going to tell her why she'd been selected out of the dozens of women he knew, she carried on searching to find the answer herself, the answer he wasn't revealing. 'You obviously need to take someone with you on Saturday—which means that you don't want to go on your own.'

'Carry on the way you're going and I'll have to promote you from Watson to Holmes,' he commented dryly.

She was not to be put off. He was a man of the world, for goodness' sake, used to going places on his own. So there had to be a reason why he wanted a woman in tow. 'You need a female partner. Someone fairly presentable and—'

'You're beautiful, and you know it,' Saul cut in, and her heart did that peculiar skip again. Did he really think her beautiful?

Realising that he had sidetracked her, Elyss determinedly got back on course again. 'Beautiful and presentable,' she commented dryly. 'And someone who...' He didn't want to go to bed with her, and he—suddenly, it clicked. 'You don't want any complications, do you?' she questioned. He didn't answer, but kept his cool glance on her alive face. Elyss, certain she had got it right, ploughed on. 'You need to go to this party on Saturday with some presentable—and, if possible, beautiful—female on your arm. Someone who knows how to behave socially, but also someone who won't complicate the issue as any one of your lady-friends might by thinking you're taking them to a party for their benefit.'

His answer was to stare at her mockingly. 'Did I mention you had a lively mind? Make that lively and fertile.'

'I'm right, though, aren't I?'

He neither confirmed nor denied. But did say, 'Why?'

'I haven't worked that out yet,' Elyss had to own.

'Let's hope the answer you dream up is less dramatic than what you've dreamed up so far,' he remarked, and asked pleasantly, patently not expecting her to reply, 'Shall we go.'

Bossy devil, she chafed to herself crossly, and felt decidedly off him—not that she'd ever been on—as he escorted her out of the hotel. Elyss felt she had nothing she wanted to say to Saul Pendleton as the doorman hailed a taxi.

She turned slightly as a taxi drew up, however, prepared to utter what she could in the way of a civilised goodnight. But when Saul bent his head, much in the manner of someone about to kiss her cheek in farewell, all pretence of trying to observe civilities abruptly fled.

'Don't even *think* about it!' she snapped, jerking away, and heard him laugh! To kiss her, it seemed, had never been in his mind. He had merely been going to open the cab door.

Elyss climbed into the taxi feeling no end of a fool. 'Seven-thirty, my place,' he commanded, and, evidently not considering that she might argue, he closed the door. She stopped feeling a fool and wanted to smack the party-ordering swine's face instead.

She switched her attention to the driver in front. But discovered she had no need to instruct him where to take her because Saul had already done so. She saw her host pay him, and as the taxi moved off she looked away. She was dammed if she was going to offer a pretty thank-you for her dinner.

Her flatmates were all in bed when she got in. She left early the next morning in order to get to work on time. So it wasn't until the next evening, after a busy day at her office, that Elyss saw Louise, who was on her way out as Elyss arrived home.

'How did last night go?' Louise asked.

Elyss wasn't terribly sure how it had gone, so settled for, 'Negotiations were amicable.'

On Wednesday Elyss began to find it very trying having to go all around the houses on public transport to get to work, so she rang the garage to enquire how the repairs to her car were going along.

'We've put on a spurt with your job,' the service manager informed her cheerfully. 'You'll be able to pick it up tomorrow. After four?'

'Great,' she replied, and put the phone down knowing she should have asked him how close he'd been able to stick to his verbal estimate. She had a feeling that his assessment had been much too modest. She worked late that night—she would be leaving early tomorrow.

With Saturday coming closer and closer, Elyss went to work on Thursday wishing with all she had that Saul Pendleton would phone to say that the party was cancelled, or that he had changed his mind about going. But the only calls she took were business calls.

She left work to go and pick up her car, reflecting that bossy Saul Pendleton had ordered her to be at his home at seven-thirty on Saturday; it was something, she supposed, that he wasn't insisting on picking her up. Nikki had seemed to be a fraction calmer when they'd shared a pot of coffee last night, but it still wouldn't take very much to make her all apprehensive and agitated again. Just a glimpse of Saul Pendleton, despite his fairly good looks, would do it.

All thoughts of Nikki, work, and Saul Pendleton went shooting from Elyss's mind when at four-forty-five that afternoon she walked into the service bay of Prompt Motor Services. She saw her car at once. The service manager was on the phone. She went over to her car, approaching it from the rear—and tried with all she had to hold down her panic. Her car was immaculate!

There was not a bump or a dent there at all. Not so much as a scratch! No sign whatsoever of the misshapen front and side that had been painfully visible the last time she had seen it. Oh, my sainted aunt! I can't afford this! she thought. It was out of the question.

'You've put a new wing on and knocked out, re-sprayed and, and...' she gasped, barely managing to keep her tone from rising when the service manager came over.

He seemed not a bit put out to be so accused, and actually smiled. 'That's right,' he answered cheerfully, 'Your—friend—rang on Tuesday and gave instructions to...'

'My *friend*?' Elyss queried, realising as she spoke that the service manager must have received instructions about someone else's car, and made a mistake. Oh, crumbs, she didn't need this. She doubted she could even afford to come to some financial agreement with him.

She was shaken out of such thoughts, however, when, as cheerful as ever, the service manager replied, 'Your friend Mr Pendleton. He phoned personally and...'

'Mr Pendleton rang you about my car?' Her tone *had* risen. Well, whose wouldn't?

'He gave instructions—it's as good as new under the bonnet too—as per his instructions. Come and take a look.'

What she would really have liked to do was to go and take a knife and slit somebody's throat! Somebody who owned the initials S.P. How could he have done what he had? How dared he? She couldn't afford the beauty work! She had as good as told him that. She clearly remembered telling him that the dents would take a little longer. Oh, how dared he do this?

'Er, you didn't—um—quote for the body work,' she began, as a prelude to telling the service manager she couldn't pay him, as she stood with him looking at the car's innards—which meant very little to her.

'Mr Pendleton said not to bother, but to get on with it with all speed.' Elyss was busy with lady-like thoughts of poking one Mr Saul Pendleton in the eye with a very sharp stick—interfering swine! But, outwardly, she was totally dumbstruck. The service manager closed the lid on the engine compartment, and added, 'I rang him this morning to say it would be ready today and what the cost of everything would be—he sent a messenger over with a cheque.' Feeling winded, scandalised and alto-gether still lost for words, Elyss searched to find her voice as the man added, 'The keys are in the ignition; you can take her any time you like.'

Elyss was on her way home, driving on automatic pilot, when it dawned on her that she hadn't asked how much the whole of the repair had cost. She decided that she didn't want to know. She just couldn't afford it.

Reaching her flat, she parked her car in her usual place and went in. She was the first one home. She had only just put the kettle on, though, when Nikki came in.

'You've got your car back!' she exclaimed, obviously having spotted it. 'W-was it fearfully costly,' she asked nervously.

What could she say? The doctor had said Nikki was not fit for work and had given her a note so she could claim state sickness benefit, and, though she seemed to be better than she had been, Elyss didn't want her going backwards in her recovery. 'Not so much,' she smiled.

'You can have my sickness benefit,' Nikki offered—and then Louise could go without her rent. 'And I'll get a j-job soon,' she said, starting to look a touch tearful.

'Of course you will,' Elyss told her bracingly. 'Though don't rush it. Wait until Dr Lowe says you're ready. Tea?'

They were sitting drinking tea when Nikki asked unhappily, 'What are we going to do, Elyss?'

Elyss wished she could tell her. The whole thing was a nightmare. 'There's nothing to do,' she lied cheerfully. 'My car repairs didn't cost as much as I thought, so I won't need your sickness benefit. And S... Mr Pendleton was most reasonable when I spoke to him on the phone.'

'He terrified me!' Nikki uttered on a scared breath.

'Well, I expect anybody would be a little bit fierce after somebody had crashed into them,' Elyss pointed out reasonably, but saw from her flatmate's worried expression that just talking about Saul Pendleton was having an adverse effect on her. 'So, what have you been doing today? Have you been getting out and taking exercise as Dr Lowe said you should?'

'I went for a walk both this morning and this afternoon,' Nikki replied—and stared into space, lost in her own thoughts. Elyss feared that Nikki's walk had included a bus ride in the direction of Dave's place too, but she felt it would be kinder not to say so.

She sipped her tea, the errant Dave forgotten, Saul Pendleton taking his place in her thoughts. What the dickens did he think he was playing at? It would be impossible for her to find the money she would already owe him once he got his car back, for repairs and car hire. She just didn't need to be further in debt for her own car repairs—heavens above, she'd never be free of him!

It worried her, so much so that around nine o'clock that night she took the phone into her room, found his card, and rang his home number. This needed sorting out—and there was no time like the present. The only problem was that he was not in. Or, if he was, he wasn't answering his phone.

Nor was he in on Friday night when she rang either. So why did he need her to go to some party with him. All too plainly he was out with a different female every night of the week.

Feeling decidedly out of sorts, Elyss went to bed. For two pins, she wouldn't go to the wretched party. She wished! She didn't have any choice. She got up on Saturday morning, and as she and her flatmates sat around drinking tea, and Victoria told them of her latest man, and Louise and Nikki invited Elyss to go to the cinema with them that night, Elyss knew that the moment she had delayed could be put off no longer.

'Actually, I'm—er—going to a party tonight,' she announced.

'It's that same man you went out with on Monday, isn't it?' Victoria pounced.

'As it happens,' Elyss agreed, and for no reason on this earth felt herself blushing. Trauma, she told herself, it's all from the trauma of recent events.

'I haven't blushed since I was sixteen!' sharp-eyed Victoria exclaimed, and received a baleful look from Louise for her lack of tact.

'Which doesn't surprise any of us!' Nikki dropped in sarcastically, and Victoria beamed.

'Hey, Nik—you're feeling better! You haven't been catty to me in ages.'

'I'm sorry.'

'Don't for pity's sake apologise.' Victoria laughed, and, looking more pleased than offended, she turned to Elyss. 'So, okay, you're not going to tell us his name—what are you going to wear?'

Elyss wondered pretty much the same herself. But that evening at five minutes to seven she stood in front of her three flatmates wearing a sleeveless dress of silky pale peppermint-green.

'Wow!' grinned Victoria.

'Likewise,' Louise smiled.

'Oh, Elyss, you look lovely,' said Nikki quietly. And, as if desperate to do something to recompense Elyss for crashing her car, she offered, 'I've an evening purse that matches your dress exactly. You must borrow it!'

'I...' Elyss began to refuse, she already had her own evening bag which, besides a lipstick, hanky, comb and car keys, held a cheque made out to Saul Pendleton for as much as she could afford. But Nikki was already on her way to get her purse.

'Let her lend it to you,' Louise whispered.

'Is it the one Dave gave her?' Victoria questioned.

Louise said it was, and added, 'I think Nikki needs to feel that she's made some sort of sacrifice for you.'

Oh, heck. If Dave had given it to her, Nikki must hold it in precious regard. Elyss doubly did not wish to borrow it. 'It's lovely, Nikki, and an excellent match,' she said when Nikki, after giving the purse a gentle stroke, handed it to her. 'Are you sure?'

'It would please me if you'd take it,' she smiled.

A few minutes later, having switched the contents of her own purse over to the one Nikki had given her, Elyss made her way to her car. She drove to Saul Pendleton's home feeling all churned up inside but still pondering why he wanted her to go with him to this wretched wedding anniversary party.

She reached his address a half-hour later, certain that her theory about him needing to take a female along who wouldn't complicate matters by thinking there was anything personal in it was correct.

Well, she jolly well knew there was nothing personal

in it. She was curious, though. Saul had asked why, when she had put her theory to him. She still hadn't worked out why.

She parked her car and went into the building where he lived. 'Miss—Harvey?' To her surprise, the security man remembered her.

'I won't go up.' She smiled. 'If you'd like to tell Mr Pendleton I'm here.'

There were a couple of sofas in the airy waiting area. Elyss went and sat down, trying to control her churning insides. A short while later she heard one of the two lifts descending. She kept her gaze averted, but as she heard the sound of the lift stopping, and the doors opening, so she just had to look.

Grief—and she'd thought him fairly good-looking! He was terrific! 'Elyss.' Saul came over, seeming taller than ever in dinner jacket, white shirt and bow tie.

'Saul,' she acknowledged, leaving the sofa. Whatever disharmony lay between them, instinctive good manners decreed that no casual observer, or, in this case, the security man, should know it. 'Will my car be all right? I've left it...'

'Bernard will move it for you.' He held his hand out for her car keys. She opened Nikki's purse, saw the cheque she intended to give him, and handed over her keys. Saul had a brief conversation with Bernard, and then he was escorting her from the building and into his car.

'Another Ferrari,' slipped unexpectedly from between her lips when Saul joined her in the gleamingly beautiful vehicle.

'Why change the habits of a lifetime?' he commented lightly, steering away from the building.

'Have you always had money?'

'Didn't your friend Louise tell you?'

'We didn't discuss your commercial value,' Elyss replied stiffly—he was making her sound like some money-grubbing harpy!

'Just my bachelor status.'

Money-grubbing and marriage-minded harpy, she amended. 'From my observations it's no wonder to me that you're still a bachelor!' she retorted sourly—and expected him to stay silent for the rest of their journey. To her annoyance, he laughed. Contrary to her desire, her acid had amused the swine.

'How's your flatmate, by the way?' he thought to ask. 'The hysterical one,' he qualified.

'A little better since she's started taking prescribed medicine,' Elyss answered, but added urgently, 'She isn't well enough to cope with any—any unpleasantness.'

'You think me an ogre?'

'You don't want to *know* what I think,' she replied, and, ridiculously, they both laughed.

'Did I say how lovely you look?' he questioned when they had been driving in silence for a few minutes.

Several answers sprang to mind. She selected the least likely he would expect. 'For you—I made the effort,' she murmured. She glanced at him, saw his mouth twitch, but if she had again amused him he controlled any impulse to smile. 'I tried to phone you yesterday, and Thursday, actually.'

'To cancel?'

Would she dare? She was in debt to him—up to her ears. 'You rang Prompt Motor Services,' she accused, and as he slowed the car to a halt at some traffic lights she dipped into the pale peppermint-green purse. 'My cheque,' she informed him as she gave it to him. 'It's

not for the full amount. As I told you, I hadn't antici-
pated having the body work done just yet. I'll...' Something in his eyes, a kind of serious, considering look,
caused her to break off.

'You can't afford this,' he said quietly, his eyes never
leaving her beautiful blue ones, seeming to know that
she had made the cheque out to the very limits she could
afford.

'Yes, I can,' she argued, and most unexpectedly experienced a choky kind of feeling. She looked away.
'The lights are changing,' she remarked, and was glad
when they were on the move again.

Oddly, she didn't feel like squaring up to him again
after that, and Saul had little to say until he pulled up at
a manor-style house. Lights seemed to be blazing everywhere, cars lined the drive. There must be hundreds of
guests here!

Saul found a parking spot and came round to the passenger door. 'Okay?' he enquired—and she wasn't fully
sure why he was asking. Was she okay because she'd
been quiet, or was she okay because she was just about
to be thrust into a whole load of strangers?

'Fine,' she replied, but did not object at the feel of
his hand on her elbow. Acknowledging people on the
way, they walked over gravel and up steps into the house
and went in search of their hosts.

Elyss considered Roland Scott a charming man. He
was slim, white-haired and an agile sixty. His wife,
about thirty, Elyss guessed, was a stunning brunette.
Saul congratulated them both and exchanged a few
pleasantries, then Roland was asking, 'Where did this
lucky man meet you?' and Elyss could quite see why
his wife had fallen for him.

Elyss was about to reply something vague along the

lines that she and Saul had met in London, when she heard Saul answer for her. 'In a manner of speaking our paths seemed to collide.'

'Intriguing,' Madeline Scott took up, giving Saul a smile. 'Have you known each other long?'

'Long enough for me to know some of Elyss's likes and dislikes,' he replied, and, while Elyss tried to keep her expression deadpan, he continued, 'And right now I know that Elyss likes to dance.' He knew nothing of the sort!

'Lucky for you I haven't got two left feet.' She was soon at his throat when he had guided her to the area that had been cleared for dancing. As yet she hadn't sorted out why he should want to give their host and hostess the impression that they had known each other some while. He certainly didn't want them to know that this was only the third time they had met, nor that they weren't even friends, much less anything closer.

Saul was courteous, she'd give him that. Introducing her to those who stopped them to have a word. Attentively seeing to it that she had whatever refreshment she required. In fact, he was being a perfect—date.

That a 'date' he wasn't, was neither here nor there. She had hoped to find some reason as to why she was here at all.

She also danced with some very pleasant men during the evening, the bachelors among them hinting they would like to call her, and one married man, who should have known better, suggesting likewise. She dealt effectively with such overtures, and it was from her married dancing partner that she learned that this was the Scotts' first wedding anniversary.

'Good of them to invite all us lot, instead of having a private do of their own. But then our Madeline's not one to want to hide herself away,' he opined, and Elyss felt a little discomfited. She had a feeling she would only have to say one word and he would be ready and more than willing to have a jolly good gossip about their hosts.

'Very good,' she smiled, and, thankfully the music came to an end, so she was able to move away from him.

'You don't seem to be lacking for partners.' Saul appeared from nowhere to claim her.

He could talk! True, she had danced a lot, but he hadn't exactly been standing in the corner twiddling his thumbs. In fact, every time she had looked around for him when she was dancing, he'd either been chatting or dancing with some near-ravishing beauty.

'What time is it?' she asked, thinking it must be getting on for eleven. She wasn't wearing a watch. Saul was; he consulted it.

'Twenty past midnight.'

'Truly!' she exclaimed. 'I thought it was much earlier.'

'You seem to have been enjoying yourself.'

Did she sense censure there? 'Forgive me, I know I wasn't supposed to!'

Saul Pendleton stared down into her sparky eyes. 'My God, the man who finally gets you is going to land himself with a handful,' he pronounced, and, when she had nothing cutting to come back with, he enquired, 'Had enough?'

'Ready to go when you are,' she replied, just as a man about the same age as Saul approached.

'Saul, I know it's not done, but I wonder if you could spare a brief minute to discuss a moment of business?' he asked.

Elyss saw the married, ready-for-a-gossip man hovering. 'Would you excuse me?' she asked politely, and, not waiting for either of them to answer, she went and found the bedroom that was being used as a cloakroom.

She hadn't brought a coat, but she rinsed her hands in the adjoining bathroom and combed her hair. Fortunately she had the room to herself. She felt she had done sufficient dancing that evening to justify Saul's assertion that 'Elyss likes to dance'. Lying toad!

She guessed a 'brief minute to discuss a moment of business' was likely to stretch into half an hour. Since she had no wish to dance with the party gossip again, she decided to stay where she was for as long as she could.

Elyss left the room only when someone else came in. They smiled at each other. 'Super party,' the other exclaimed.

'Super,' Elyss agreed, and, hoping that Saul had finished his business, and with thoughts of looking for their host and hostess to say Thank-you and Goodbye, she went along the landing.

She reached the top of the stairs, and was musing that first she would have to find Saul when she abruptly stopped dead—in shock. She did not have to look far, she at once saw. For there was Saul at the bottom of the stairs, plainly oblivious to anyone but the woman—her hand possessively on his arm—he was standing with.

Saul was half turned from her so that Elyss could not see the whole of his expression, but there could be no doubting to anyone watching that he was on the *best* of terms with the woman who was looking so adoringly up at him. That woman, Madeline Scott! The shock of it was to know, quite unmistakably, that the two of them were having an affair!

Elyss *knew* that there had been some particular reason

for Saul ordering her to come to this party with him. But this was one reason she had not thought of! Saul Pendleton held Roland Scott in great respect, but, sickeningly, not great enough respect to stop him playing around with Roland's wife!

She had wondered why Saul had wanted to give Roland and Madeline the impression that they had known each other for some while. It was not for Madeline's benefit, Elyss now realised. Madeline probably knew all about it. It was for Roland's benefit alone. A cover, a screen for what was going on behind his back!

Elyss started to grow angry, and in doing so began to get over her shock. At that same moment both Saul and Madeline seemed to become aware that they were being observed. And Elyss grew more angry. They didn't even attempt to look guilty. Madeline still had her hand possessively on Saul's sleeve as he turned and followed her glance up the stairs. Elyss looked coldly back.

Then she became aware that the woman she had passed in the bedroom was hurrying to rejoin the party, and Elyss forced a smile. It would be great, wouldn't it, if on this, the Scotts' first wedding anniversary, anything was given away of the duplicity being practised?

Elyss went down the stairs a little behind the other woman, her gaze firmly cast downwards. 'I was just coming to find you,' Saul said smoothly as she reached him. I'll bet!, thought Elyss.

She looked up and saw that Roland had appeared from somewhere. Thank goodness he hadn't been there a minute earlier. She smiled at him; she liked him and felt hurt for him. 'Thank you for a wonderful party. The evening has simply flown,' she murmured, extending her hand.

'I can't persuade you to stay a little longer?'

'Have a heart, Roland, I've hardly had a moment alone with Elyss all evening,' Saul answered—and severely aggressive tendencies were awakened in Elyss; she felt like punching him on the jaw.

She supposed, her upbringing being what it was, she must have managed a polite 'Thank you and goodnight' to Madeline, but as she sat beside Saul on the drive back to his apartment Elyss could not remember doing so.

'You hate me, don't you?' Saul questioned, more than clever enough to have read her cold look from the top of the stairs—and the reason for it.

'You're a rat!' she answered tautly, and had nothing further to say to him until they had reached his apartment building and he had escorted her inside to pick up her car keys.

The security man handed them to her and, thanking him, she turned about. She then found that Saul was accompanying her outside to where Bernard had parked her car.

'Do I take it you're not coming up for coffee?' Saul enquired mockingly.

'You can keep your coffee!' she replied politely—and, getting into her car, she parted from him for a second time without saying goodbye.

CHAPTER FOUR

ELYSS did not sleep well. How could he? How could Saul Pendleton have an affair behind the back of the man he said he had a great respect for? Something sharp and heavy should be dropped on Saul from a mile up! And she would like to be the one who did the dropping! Saul Pendleton... She suddenly realised that it was a little bit odd that, when she hardly knew Roland Scott, she was sleepless with indignation on his behalf!

Well, it was for sure she wasn't indignant on her own behalf. As if it bothered her how many mistresses the smooth, sophisticated swine had! Anyway, didn't she have a right to be indignant? She was being used! Yes, but, she suddenly remembered, she owed him two thousand pounds plus. She groaned—no wonder she couldn't go to sleep! And she had called him a rat and told him to keep his coffee!

'I didn't expect you to surface for ages yet,' Louise commented when, insomnia her sudden enemy, Elyss joined her in the kitchen at seven on Sunday morning. 'Good party?'

'It was, actually. It was a wedding anniversary party.'

'Did you go with Saul Pendleton?'

'You guessed.'

'I wondered. Er—forgive me saying this,' Louise went on, 'but, well, from what I've heard, he eats little girls like you for breakfast.'

He wasn't interested in blonde little girls like her! He went more for sophisticated, stunning brunettes. 'I hope to be the first to give him indigestion,' Elyss smiled, 'but thanks for your concern.'

'You're seeing him again?'

From choice, no. 'It's odd,' Elyss suddenly realised, 'but, although I've been in his company several times now, I don't seem to have been able to pin him down as to what he has decided to do about the money I shall owe him. Did I tell you I've decided to try and find some weekend work?'

'Oh, so that's why you've been studying the Situations Vacant columns in the paper! I thought you were thinking of telling Howard Butler and Co goodbye. Seen anything you fancy?'

'There was only one for a barmaid in Friday's paper, but they wanted somebody experienced. I'll—' She broke off as Nikki, another recent insomniac, came to join them.

'How was your party?' she managed to find a smile to ask.

'Terrific,' Elyss beamed, and went and had a shower, her mind flitting here and there—from Saul Pendleton and his treachery, to how she must let Nikki have her evening purse back, and... She was out of the shower, towelling herself dry, when it suddenly came to her that she could not remember the last time she had seen that purse!

She returned to her room and hurriedly got dressed while, trying not to panic, she searched, without success, for the missing purse. Oh, heck, Nikki would be distraught if she had lost it! Elyss backtracked to when she could last remember having the purse in her hands. She'd definitely had it when she went upstairs to the bedroom-cloakroom at the Scotts', she recalled, but not afterwards.

Which didn't surprise her. She'd been so churned up, angry and shocked when she'd seen Madeline Scott and Saul in such obvious intimate conversation, that not much else had registered. Had she left the purse at the Scotts' home? Bernard, at Saul's place, had minded her car keys, and, since she always had her key to the flat attached to her car key ring, there had been no need for her to go into her purse for anything once she'd left the party.

I'm panicking unnecessarily, she resolved, and, taking up her car keys, she left the flat fully confident that she would find the purse where she had left it—on the passenger seat of her car. It was, after all, the natural place to put it. If the purse had been more familiar to her, her own, she'd have automatically picked it up.

She unlocked her car. The purse was not on the passenger seat. Elyss looked under the seats, in fact everywhere. It was nowhere to be seen. She strove hard for calm—Nikki would go spare; it was so precious to her, the one and only thing Dave had ever given her.

Perhaps she'd left it in Saul's car. Oh, grief—she'd have to contact him! She didn't want to contact him. She sighed and went back to the flat, picking up the phone and taking it with her into her bedroom as she went.

It was early. It was Sunday. Why should he sleep? It was about time he was up. She dialled—he didn't answer. So what kind of respectable person was out and about at this hour on a Sunday morning?

Oh, for goodness' sake. Feeling impatient with herself, impatient with Saul Pendleton and desperately anxious that she had lost Nikki's purse, Elyss went and returned the phone to its station. Louise had already left the apartment to spend some time with her son and to take him out to lunch. Victoria was having a lie-in and probably wouldn't surface before noon. But Elyss bumped into a forlorn-looking Nikki wandering around.

Guilt and compassion mingled. 'Coming for a drive, Nikki?' she invited, and, when Nikki already started to look a little brighter, 'If you fancy being really decadent, we could find a supermarket café and have a bacon and egg fry-up.' She reckoned she could run to that.

It was a little after three when they got back. Nikki's first action was to dial one four seven one to check the phone number of the last person to phone. It had not been Dave—but a friend of Victoria's who had rung last night.

No sooner had she put the phone down, though, than Elyss picked it up and took it into her room. Of the two, she felt that she was now the more tense, having feared the whole time they were out that Nikki was going to ask about her purse.

Elyss checked her watch. Three-twenty. She didn't want to talk to Saul, she really didn't. But if he wasn't home now, she could see herself still dialling his number at midnight—that or going and parking herself at his door.

She dialled, and waited, and waited. In fact she waited so long she was sure he was still out. Then the ringing tone suddenly stopped and, as her heart seemed to give an odd little leap, 'Pendleton,' Saul answered.

'I'm—er—sorry to bother you...' She hadn't thought about what she was going to say when he answered, if he answered—what was there to think about, for goodness' sake? 'Oh, it's Elyss,' she went on, only then realising that he wouldn't have a clue who was calling.

There was a moment's pause, and she suddenly had an idea that he had known at once who it was without her having said so. Then, his voice full of mockery, he drawled, 'How are you, Elyss? You know, somehow I didn't expect to hear from you again—this soon.'

Okay, so the last time she'd seen him she had told him in no uncertain terms to keep his coffee, but did he have to rub it in that at some future date there would have to be a financial reckoning? Not that she was going to apologise for her remark—playing fast and loose with other men's wives the way he was doing!

'The thing is, I've lost my evening purse. The one I had last night. Actually, it's not mine but one of Nikki's which she insisted I borrow. It has tremendous sentimental value for her, and—' Elyss broke off. What was it about this man? She was rambling again. 'Have you see it?' she asked abruptly.

'Pale green?'

That would do. 'Yes,' she replied eagerly. 'Is it...?'

'It's here.'

'Oh, thank goodness for that!' Elyss uttered, her relief heartfelt and obvious, the tension she had been under already leaving her.

'My word, it does sound important,' Saul commented. But mockery was back in his voice when he offered, 'Would you like me to drop it off at your place?'

'No, I w—' She stopped—and took a steadying breath. She could, Elyss knew, have taken his offer at face value—a kindly gesture and nothing more. But this was a man whom she knew forgot nothing—and he knew full well that she didn't want him coming anywhere near the apartment. 'Would you...?'

'Would I?' he prompted when she hesitated.

She had been going to ask if he would mind popping the purse in the post. But, now that she knew where it was she wanted hold of it with all speed. Nikki had been far more restrained in asking for it back than she might have been, but Elyss wouldn't be surprised to receive a knock on her door at any moment.

'I'd like to collect it, if I may? As soon as possible,' she tacked on—lest he gave her some date a fortnight next Wednesday.

'If you could make it before seven,' he agreed pleasantly. 'I have to go out this evening.'

For some reason that tacked-on sentence revealing that he had to go out that evening niggled her. She'd thought she didn't care a button when he went out, or with whom—though it was to be hoped that this evening's female didn't have some unsuspecting husband waiting at home. On second thoughts, a husband with a double-barrelled shotgun would be nice! Elyss abruptly brought her mind away from such pleasant visions, honour decreeing that Saul shouldn't think that the most exciting thing that went on in her life was a game of Scrabble in the evening.

'I happen to have quite a busy social life myself,' she informed him coolly.

'You've got a date?'

A simple question. So how did he manage to make it sound as though she stayed in nights as though she never dated? 'I'm a normal woman for goodness' sake!' she retorted—she should have hit him last night when he was close enough.

'Of course you are,' he answered soothingly. Soothingly? 'Yet… Why are you still—unawakened?' he had the nerve to want to know.

'When I look at types like you, I know why!' she erupted angrily. As she heard his light—and was it triumphant?—laugh she realised that until she had just

confirmed it, he had only suspected that she was a virgin.
Now he knew!

Furiously she disconnected her call, feeling hostile to
the telephone company and the progress made in its
equipment. It would have relieved her feelings somewhat
to have been able to slam the phone down. Much more
satisfying than merely pressing a plastic button.

So much for her wanting to make him feel like a
worm, when she'd retorted with 'types like you'. He'd
laughed. The swine had laughed! But if she wanted that
purse back—she had to go and see him!

There was no way she was going to ring him again.
But, oh, how she wished that she had suggested that he
gave the purse to the man on the security desk. All she
would have to do then would be to drive over, pop in
to pick it up and hey presto— 'Thanks very much,
Nikki, for loaning me your purse.' As it was, she was
going to have to see Saul again. Face him...

Elyss halted, amazed at the way her thoughts were
going. Grief—anyone would think she was afraid to face
him! Rubbish! Without more ado, pausing only to check
that her jeans and T-shirt were acceptable to go calling—
she wouldn't be stopping long enough to have to make
an alternative selection from her wardrobe—Elyss ran a
comb through her hair and, returning the phone whence
it came, she went in search of Nikki.

'Just nipping out for an hour or so; if my mother
rings...' she smiled.

'I'll cover for you,' Nikki assured her, although that
wasn't quite what Elyss had meant in telling her. She
went out to her car, only then realising how different her
relationship with her mother and father was from those
of her flatmates with their parents.

Or was it? While managing not to tell outright lies,

one or other of them seemed often to be hiding from
their parents any of their activities that might cause pa-
rental worry. But they had never had to cover for *her*
before.

The accident had changed all that. She had been a
tinge evasive herself with her parents recently, she recalled, and had decided that when next she drove down
to Devon and they saw the bashed-in bonnet of her car,
to prevent them being over anxious she would have to
tell them that Nikki had been at the wheel when it had
happened. But she had resolved not to reveal her lack
of insurance cover and the massive debt she was going
to owe the other driver. Now that Saul had taken it on
himself to have her car repaired there seemed little point
in worrying her parents with any of it. So—it was,
Welcome to the Deceive Your Parents club.

Elyss was not feeling very pleased with herself when
she parked her car and went into Saul's apartment building. Bernard gave her a smart, 'Good Afternoon, Miss
Harvey,' as she confidently stepped by, but made no
attempt to detain her as she went over to the lifts.

No doubt Saul had phoned down and advised him that
if she arrived before seven he would condescend to see
her. But then, she wasn't feeling very pleased with Saul
Pendleton either.

In fact, having ridden up in a lift, and having rung his
doorbell, she was most very definitely anti-Saul
Pendleton when the door opened and she saw not only
him but her hostess of last evening!

This confirmation that he was having an affair with
his chairman's wife made Elyss want to turn straight
around and get out of there. She felt a sick kind of feeling in the pit of her stomach. She had never thought of
herself as a prude, but this—and Lord knew how long

Madeline had been there—made her feel distinctly angry
with the pair of them.

'You know Madeline.' Saul was the first to speak—
with not a shred of embarrassment about him—as
Madeline Scott, on her way out, it appeared, stepped out
into the hall.

Never had manners been more called upon. 'Hello,
Madeline. I enjoyed your party,' a well-brought-up Elyss
found from somewhere.

Her manners, she discovered, were not required. For
Madeline, elegant, soignée and dressed to kill, merely
nodded in the direction of Elyss's jeans and T-shirt. Saul
courteously going with her to press the button of the
waiting lift, Madeline passed by Elyss.

Elyss had a fleeting impression that Madeline seemed
a trifle upset about something. Perhaps she wasn't
pleased that Elyss had arrived and broken up her 'tête-
à-tête'—that was one description for it!—with Saul. Certainly Madeline would have preferred not to be found in
her lover's apartment at four o'clock in the afternoon.
Well, she needn't have left on Elyss's account. Just give
me that purse, and I'll be off, thought Elyss.

She did not presume to enter his apartment until, his
adieu made to his departed love, Saul came back to her.
'Come in,' he invited, and seemed on top of the world.
And why wouldn't he?

It was that last thought that did it. He'd just spent a
pleasant Sunday, hadn't he? The cheating swine. *And*
with another date scheduled for seven o'clock.

'Your girlfriend needn't have left because of me!'
Elyss fired acidly, having not wanted to say anything,
but seeming unable to hold her tart words in.

Saul halted in the middle of his drawing room carpet,
one eyebrow going slightly aloft. 'That's very generous

of you, Elyss,' he drawled silkily—his sarcasm causing her to feel about as big as tuppence. That annoyed her. *She'd* done nothing wrong!

'I rang you first thing this morning!' was the best retort she could find, her tone accusatory—who the devil did he think he was?—him and his sarcasm!

'And I missed you,' he answered, and suddenly she felt certain that he was laughing at her. 'I must have been down in the pool.'

Naturally they'd have a gym in the salubrious apartment block, and a swimming pool—pity he hadn't drowned! 'It wasn't you particularly that I wanted, but Nikki's purse!' Elyss set him straight. She hadn't expected him to look desolate at the fact that the purse was of more interest to her than he was—which was just as well, for he looked more ready to laugh than to cry. 'May I have it please?' she requested primly.

'Of course,' he answered obligingly, and went from the drawing room to wherever it was to get it.

Elyss had but a minute or so while he was away in which to give herself a talking to. Why was she behaving like this for goodness' sake? It was nothing to her how many mistresses he had, married or otherwise. Nor how many men he much respected, but whom he was still prepared to metaphorically stab in the back. *And*, don't forget, you still owe him over two thousand pounds! a small voice in her head reminded her.

'Saul,' she said quickly when he returned, 'about the money I owe you...'

He came close up to her, and looked down into her earnest blue eyes. He smiled and her heart did a peculiar sort of flip. 'One thing at a time, little Elyss,' he said, quite pleasantly, tapping her nose with a long sensitive finger. 'I'll be in touch,' he added, and handed over the

one thing they were dealing with at this particular time—
Nikki's purse.

'Of course, you're going out,' she remembered, realising it wasn't convenient for him just now to have any
discussion in depth—not that it would take three hours!

'As are you,' he replied, and for one awful moment
she thought that was his way of saying, You've got what
you came for, now clear off—until she remembered that
she'd as good as told him she had a date herself that
night.

'That's true,' she lied, and turned from him towards
the door in case her cheeks had gone a little pink. 'Thank
you for the purse. Nikki will be glad to see it again,'
she trotted out as he walked with her across the carpet,
finding that she was having to make an effort to hold
down more words that sprang to her lips—she felt a very
real danger of rambling. 'I'll—er—wait to hear from you
when you're ready,' she said at the door, and, when it
seemed that he had said all that he wanted to say, she
gulped, 'Bye then,' and got out of there.

Elyss drove home wondering what on earth was the
matter with her. She parked her car, coming to the conclusion that there was not a thing wrong with her, for
heaven's sake. It was just that she was under a little
stress about that money—who wouldn't be? And that,
while having obeyed his order to go with him to that
party last night might have paid off a little of the debt,
even if she charged a partying rate of an excessive
twenty pounds an hour, she still had barely started to
pay off what she owed.

It was worse than that, she discovered, when back up
in her room, she went to empty out the purse prior to
handing it back to Nikki. In tipping out the contents onto

her bed, along with her lipstick, comb and hanky, the cheque she had last night given Saul fell out too!

What the dickens was he playing at? So, all right, he knew she could barely afford the amount she had written, but this was ridiculous. How was she ever going to clear what she owed him if he made a practice of giving her her cheques back?

Elyss felt angry with him again and felt very much like telephoning him. But he was going out. She did not ring him. And although she felt like ringing him every day in the week that followed, she did not do so.

Nor did he call her at work, when she'd expected that he might. Quite clearly it was taking him a long time to decide what to do about the money she would end up owing him when his car was repaired. Though, on thinking about it, and she seldom stopped, she was never going to be able to afford to repay him anyway. So, on balance, since he knew what she earned—and probably had a fair idea of her outgoings too—no wonder it was taking so long for Saul to work out what was to be done about it.

She spent the following weekend quietly. Louise had gone to stay with her parents for a week. Victoria and Nikki went out together both on Saturday and Sunday. 'Come with us,' Nikki invited, improving slowly, but still under medical supervision.

Elyss was in a pensive mood, and wasn't keen. 'Some other time,' she smiled, and had Saul Pendleton much on her mind all weekend. And not, she realised with surprise when she lay in her bed on Sunday night, solely because of that car crash and its financial consequences. What was he doing? Who was he doing it with? How long had his affair with Madeline Scott been going on? Didn't Roland have any inkling?

She awakened to a cold, raining Monday, and Saul was still in her head when she went to work. It was obvious to her that he dated other women as well as carrying on his affair. Didn't Madeline mind? Not that she could have any axe to grind—she had a husband she went home to at night—presumably.

Saul Pendleton did not ring her at work that day either. Elyss knew he would not ring her at home— should Nikki chance to answer the phone then she would only need to hear his commanding voice and all the progress she had made in this last couple of weeks could come to nothing.

It was still damp and overcast when Elyss left her office that night. She left on time for once, and was swinging into the firm's car park with William from Purchasing when William's sudden exclamation caused her to turn her glance to where he was looking.

'Now *that's* what I call a car!' he exclaimed in over-awed tones.

Elyss could not believe it. Of course there was more than one Ferrari in the world but... The driver's door opened, a tall, dark-haired man got out—and waited. He'd obviously been watching for her.

This was embarrassing! 'I'll see you tomorrow, William,' she bade him goodbye, more in hope than expectation that he would go over to his own car and drive off.

But, it wasn't every day, or any day, that a Ferrari of such superb modelling was parked in Howard Butler and Co's car park. Nor was William the only car-mad male who stopped dead to admire its sleek lines. Elyss saw Ivor and Johnny from Sales, and Kevin from Salaries, all come to a sudden and appreciative halt.

Oh, Lord, she groaned silently, balancing up her op-

tions. She either had to go and say hello to Saul
Pendleton or ignore him completely and go straight to
her car. Since it was plain Saul was there to talk to her,
he might shoot out of the car park after her—clearly
following her.

She went over to him. 'Thanks, for nothing!' she
snapped.

And knew he was as sharp on the uptake as ever
when, with a glance to the audience, he invited pleasantly, 'Get in. We'll go for a drive.'

Elyss didn't want to go for a drive. But she got in,
and as they sailed out of the firm's car park she kept her
eyes down, her shoulder bag now on her lap and of great
interest.

'Your phone not working?' she challenged snappily,
once they were away from interested eyes.

'I did think of calling at your address to see you,' he
replied curtly, and Elyss gave him a withering look.

Which, of course, since he had his eyes on the road
in front of him, was entirely wasted. This, she realised,
was it. Saul had spent more than a week mulling over
what was to be done for the best. He had now reached
his conclusion and, since he must know that she was no
more likely to have the cash for him this week than she
had been last week, it was time to have a chat. By the
look of it, a chat in person, where she could not, should
she feel like it, simply terminate the conversation by the
push of a plastic button.

Not that she would have anyway. But now she was
not in that fortunate position. Saul drove out of London
but drew up in the first patch of countryside they came
to. It had come on to rain again, which might have been
the reason why he did not suggest they got out of the
car and walked. But Elyss, starting to feel very wary,

had an uncanny sensation that he wanted her captive in his car while he told her what he had decided. He turned to look at her, his steady grey eyes making a thorough scrutiny of her face.

'You shouldn't have returned my cheque!' she blurted out in a rush of nervousness. 'I'm never going to be out of your debt if you play tricks like that!'

'You're not frightened of me?' he demanded abruptly—appearing not to like that notion one tiny bit.

She didn't have to think about it. 'Of course I'm not,' she scoffed.

'You seem nervous,' he qualified.

'I suppose I'm—' She broke off; she wasn't sure herself what she was. 'I'm a—er—little edgy. I owe you money, can't pay you—well not straight away—but you've obviously come up with some scheme.' Elyss was about to charge on to state how she'd raise a bank loan if she could only, but she hadn't any collateral and she'd be laughed out of the bank when she detailed her incomings and her outgoings. She was, she knew, on the brink of rambling again. She took a deep breath, and plunged. 'So?'

'So?' he encouraged—was he being maddening on purpose?

'So, given that I haven't paid for as much as a door lock on your car by going to that party with you the Saturday before last—not that I take very kindly to being used as cover for the affair you're having—' She broke off, holding back more words—she couldn't afford to be high-minded.

'Ye gods, a woman with morals!' Saul mocked.

'You've been mixing with the wrong types!' she flew. Oh, grief—where had that temper come from? She hadn't used to be like this. It was all his fault, of course.

She took another deep breath, waited until she felt she was more in control, and quietly stated, 'Actually, it's my turn to cook the meal at the flat tonight. If you wouldn't mind…'

'See, you *can* ask nicely if you want to.' She was going to hit him. One of these days she was going to have the unmitigated delight of punching his head in.

'So?' she asked, trying hard not to grind her teeth.

Saul looked at her. Studied her. And Elyss knew darn well that she wasn't going to like it—and that was before, as nice as you please, he affably announced, 'I need a—woman-friend, for a few days.'

Her breath caught. She knew that there was more behind it than he was stating, but she wasn't interested in hearing what. 'What's the matter, Pendleton,' she erupted, 'your charm failing?' She didn't even dent him. In fact, he grinned, and that annoyed her. 'What's wrong with the woman you've already got?'

'Were you always such a lippy shrew?' he asked pleasantly.

'You bring out the best in me!'

'It's a gift I have,' he mocked, but was totally serious when he went on to set it out for her. 'In return for you giving me five days of your time, I, for my part, am prepared to cancel all present and future debts in relation to repairs to your vehicle and to mine.'

Elyss stared at him dumbstruck. Just like that he was offering to let her off paying her debt to him—if she gave him five days of her time! There had to be a catch! 'You—want me to give you five days of my time?' Solemn-eyed, she faced him. It sounded good—brilliant wasn't overstating it—she knew it couldn't be that simple. 'What's the snag—accepting that I'd have to put up with you five days?' she queried warily.

She saw his mouth move almost imperceptibly, as though she made him want to smile. He didn't smile, though, but stated, 'I said I needed a "woman-*friend*"; I didn't mean enemy.'

'I can be a friend,' she said. 'To be free of a debt of two thousand pounds plus, I can be a jolly good friend. But I still need to know more.'

'Of course you do,' he agreed, and that again made her wary. She was getting not to trust him when he was being affable. 'Not long ago,' he began to outline, 'Roland Scott bought a villa on a remote Greek island.' Fascinating—but where did she come in? 'The more he spoke of how little there was on the island, except for a few other villas, the odd goat-herd and a stray taverna, the more I thought it sounded the ideal place to unwind.' It did sound rather good, she had to admit. 'I said as much, and Roland insisted that at the first opportunity I should spend some time there.'

Here we go! Snag number one had just raised its ugly head, though in this case it was a rather beautiful brunette head. 'I'm still with you,' Elyss encouraged—a shade coolly, she had to admit. If her vibes were right, she was streets ahead!

'Roland and Madeline have managed to spend time on Kafros, of course, but I never have.' He paused, then added succinctly, 'Until now.'

'You're going now, to Kafros, this island?' Elyss queried, she'd lost him somewhere—and she'd been tuned in to his every word.

'Oak International have been negotiating a deal with the Georgoulis Company, a Greek company,' Saul continued. 'Details will be completed today, and Roland and I are going over to finalise everything and take a few days' holiday.'

'With Madeline, naturally.' Elyss had just caught up.

'She'll stay on the island on Thursday while Roland and I go to Athens.'

'No!' Elyss said promptly.

'No, what?'

'No, I'm not coming.' Cheeky swine. The nerve of him. He thought he could take her, his 'woman-friend', as a cover for what he wanted to get up to with his colleague's wife. He could go take a running jump into the Aegean! 'That's what you're asking, isn't it? Me to go with you?'

Saul nodded and studied her mutinous expression. Then he smiled. She didn't trust that smile either. And knew she was right not to trust him when, silkily, he let fall, 'Loath though I am to mention it—you *do* owe me.'

'You're a pig!' she raged impotently. 'And I hate you,' she added for good furious measure.

'Well, that's a nice friendly start.'

'Look here, Mister!' she flew. 'If you think I'm coming to some Greek island with you so you can use me as a screen while you play—play—bouzoukis with Roland Scott's wife, you can...' She came to an abrupt halt when Saul burst out laughing. Oh—she so nearly hit him!

'Wash out your mouth!' he instructed, but was serious when he informed her, 'I hold Roland in too high a regard to want to play anything with his wife.'

'While he's around!' Elyss retorted—and witnessed the kind of expression on Saul's face which she would imagine he wore in the boardroom when he needed to get tough.

He had certainly done with 'asking nicely' anyhow, when, his chin jutting, he demanded curtly, 'To hell with it—are you coming or not?'

'Not!' she hurled back. But, after giving her a swift, cutting look, he otherwise ignored her and went to switch on the car's ignition.

'The alternatives are that either I go to Greece with you or you'll be round at my place looking for Nikki—with a view to summonsing her—quicker than a rat—' she chose the term with care '—down a sewer pipe.'

Humour he didn't seem to want tugged at the corners of his mouth at her 'rat' description. 'That seems a fair assessment.'

Swine. 'When do you need to know by?'

Rain lashed the windscreen. 'Sun, sea, a holiday! It needs thinking about?'

Not to reiterate she'd be out of his debt at the end of it! 'Rest your case—I'll ring you.'

He turned the key. The engine started at once.

Saul returned her to the car park of Howard Butler and Company. Even while Elyss was fighting against going with him to Greece she knew she was going to have to give in. Apart from the money involved, Nikki would just flip if Saul came ringing their doorbell. But Elyss, stubbornly, wasn't ready to give in yet.

'When do you leave?' she questioned tautly.

'Wednesday.'

Elyss reached for the doorhandle. 'I'll ring you,' she repeated, and left him.

He waited to see her drive out of the car park—she didn't thank him for the courtesy. She reached the flat and found Victoria was too busy coping with a heart-broken Nikki to have noticed she was late home.

'What's wrong?' Elyss whispered, and discovered that Nikki had called on the indescribable Dave that lunch-time. The door had been answered by his live-in girl-friend.

Men!

Elyss made a meal which only Victoria felt like eating, and after washing up and generally tidying around took the phone into her bedroom. She would have to have time off from work—at this short notice she wouldn't be popular. But thank goodness it wasn't her father's birthday until a week next Saturday. She'd be back in plenty of time for that—there was nothing to stop her from going.

Get it over with. Phone him. Some stubbornness made Elyss hold back from stabbing out those digits of Saul's number. She had very mixed feelings about spending five days in his company. She felt all stewed up inside as she recalled his grey-eyed, good-looking face. Oh, she knew that there was nothing personal in it. For five days he needed... She stopped abruptly, her thoughts shooting up a totally different avenue. Five days—he had said nothing about the nights!

Feeling more churned up than ever, Elyss went back over her recent conversation with Saul until she came to what amounted to a denial that he *was* having an affair with Madeline Scott. 'I hold Roland in too high a regard to want to...' he'd said. Could she believe that?

He seemed a sincere sort of man, but... Oh, for heaven's sake! Hadn't she seen Saul and Madeline at that wretched party—Madeline looking adoringly up at him, her hand intimately on his arm, Saul, not objecting in the slightest, looking down at her? And had she forgotten the following afternoon, when she had gone over to pick up Nikki's purse? He'd been 'entertaining' Madeline in his apartment then, hadn't he? So why, Elyss wondered, did she think Saul wanted her to go to Greece with them if it wasn't as a cover?

If it wasn't as a cover? Oh, her sainted aunt, she must

have cracked under the strain of trying to think up ways to get the money she owed him together. Why, if he wasn't having an affair with Madeline, would he want to pay her what amounted to two thousand pounds plus to go along?

A half an hour later and Elyss was still puzzling at it. She had originally thought, when Saul had invited her to go to that party with him—invited, did she say? Ordered her to go to that party!—that he had wanted to take her along to make some female jealous. But, since there seemed to be only the four of them going to Greece, and, if she accepted for the moment that Saul was not having an affair with Madeline—where did that leave her?

Her head was beginning to ache. Elyss gave it up. She was certain that she was being used as a cover but— with a wisp of doubt floating about—what if she wasn't? She gave a strangled sound of pure exasperation, and, taking up the phone, pressed out Saul's number.

'Pendleton,' he answered almost at once—so he wasn't otherwise engaged!

Elyss opened her mouth and, without announcing who she was, got straight to the point. 'This Greek thing,' she said shortly, leaving him to guess who was calling. 'I'm not sleeping with you!'

He knew who it was; she knew he did. Even if there was a light pause before he answered. 'I know you say that to all the boys, Elyss…' He broke off, and she knew he was laughing at her when he added, 'But when did I ask?'

She refused to feel humiliated. So, okay, she wasn't his type, and he didn't fancy her—as if she cared! But, since she couldn't see any alternative but to go with him, she saw nothing wrong in getting the sleeping arrangements established before she agreed to lift so much as a toe off English soil.

'What time on Wednesday?' she demanded in a friendly manner.

'Morning. Get here for nine,' he ordered, and, taking her agreement as read, he terminated the call.

Overbearing swine. To terminate the call was supposed to be her prerogative!

CHAPTER FIVE

TUESDAY passed in one big rush. First Elyss had to see her boss and arrange to have the next three days off. By her reckoning, and the devil could take it that there was no way she was going to ring Saul Pendleton again, her five days of purgatory ended on Sunday.

Having arranged to take the time off, she then rushed about, getting her desk shipshape for when she saw it again next Monday. In her lunch-hour she shopped for essentials for some days in the sun.

She was interrupted several times during her day when male visitors, William from Purchasing, Ivor, Johnny and Kevin, all casually dropped by to comment, 'Now that's what I call a car', or similar, and she had to rush a bit more to make up for time lost.

She arrived home later than she had wanted and found Nikki once more getting herself back together again. She was cooking the meal.

'Can I leave you to it?' Elyss asked; in normal times Nikki wasn't very co-ordinated in the kitchen—heaven alone knew what time they'd eat. 'I'd like to go and pack.'

'Pack! You're going away?'

'Only for a few days.'

'Devon?'

'Er—no.' Oh, grief—her parents! 'Um—I wouldn't—er—my mother might ring this weekend. I...'

'Say no more,' Victoria chimed in, 'leave it with us.' Elyss was starting to feel quite dreadful about deceiving her parents. 'We wouldn't mind knowing the boyfriend's name, though, would we Nik?' Victoria hinted.

Oh, yes, you would! Elyss smiled, and shook her head. Victoria, like the good soul she was, did not pursue it.

Elyss was up early on Wednesday morning, and was striving desperately to view this little jaunt more as the holiday Saul had described than the dreadful time she felt sure it was going to be.

On thinking about it, Elyss felt sure that she would have had enough of Saul Pendleton by the time she returned. For that reason she splashed out on a taxi to his home, rather than take her car and have to endure more of his company than necessary when they landed on Sunday; she would take a taxi home from the airport— no need for Saul to give her a lift back to her car.

It was not Bernard who was on duty when the taxi dropped her off at Saul's apartment building, but someone equally efficient.

'Would you let Mr Pendleton know I'm here?' she requested. She was very conscious of her suitcase and the fact that when Saul arrived he would be carrying a suitcase too; it wouldn't take Bernard's colleague a minute to assume that they were off somewhere together.

Saul did not keep her waiting when, suitcase and briefcase in hand, he joined her. 'Morning Elyss,' he greeted her—and dropped a light kiss on her cheek.

'Cut that out!' she snapped, certain that the jumping up and down of her stomach was because she didn't like to be so greeted.

'Sweet child,' Saul breathed teasingly, and, while Elyss was acknowledging that, well, yes, perhaps she might have overreacted a tiny bit, he continued, 'We'll garage your car and—'

'I came by taxi,' she butted in—and before she knew it was in Saul's Ferrari on her way to the airport.

Madeline Scott was agreeable, without being warm, and Roland Scott was every bit as nice as Elyss remembered him. Observing for herself how easily he and Saul got on with each other, Elyss started to wonder if perhaps she had got it wrong. Perhaps Saul and Madeline were not having an affair, for how could any man be so two-faced? How could he behave with Roland in such a friendly, honourable way, and be dishonourable behind Roland's back?

Such thoughts occupied a good deal of Elyss's time. This was her first time on a private jet and, she considered, the return flight would definitely be her last. The plane headed for Greece.

If Madeline and Saul weren't having an affair, though, if there was no relationship, then Saul would not need her presence as cover. So, why *had* he brought her along?

It wasn't just for her company; she could be sure of that. Grief, from what Louise had said, Elyss was aware that Saul knew at least any one of a dozen women who would jump at the chance of a few days, five, to be precise, on some Greek island, *without* him having to offer the inducement of debt clearance.

Ah! A notion suddenly came to her that perhaps because Roland and Madeline had only been married a year, Saul didn't want to play gooseberry. Elyss warmed to her theme. Perhaps *that* was why Saul had invited her along. He must have felt he needed a 'woman-friend' of his own—just as he'd said. But he didn't want to bring along any female he knew, in case she got the wrong idea.

Elyss remembered thinking something similar before,

when Saul had asked her to attend that party. But then she also remembered Madeline's possessive hold on Saul's arm at the party, the adoring looks, the sense of intimacy. And Madeline had been familiar enough to be coming out of Saul's apartment the next day when Elyss had gone to pick up Nikki's purse.

Elyss gave it up. Her head was starting to spin so much, she didn't know what she believed any more. All she could do, she decided, was to be watchful. Roland was such a delightful man that she just could not bear it if Madeline and Saul were to so treacherously deceive him. Though what she was going to do about it she had no idea.

They landed in Greece to wonderful sunshine. 'I suggest lunch first, and then to Kafros,' Roland declared, in such high and happy spirits that Elyss knew that if there was anything amiss with his marriage, he did not have the first inkling of it.

'That sounds lovely, darling,' Madeline agreed.

'Elyss?' Saul asked.

'Sounds good,' she replied, finding she liked his courtesy.

Lunch went very smoothly, and, to her surprise, Elyss discovered that when they strolled around the harbour afterwards, she quite like being paired off with Saul, as she and he walked in front and Madeline and Roland ambled along behind them.

She didn't know quite how she felt, however, when, almost imperceptibly—she felt a frisson of electricity shoot up her arm—Saul took her small hand in his manly one!

Elyss owned to feeling a little taken aback. But if Saul Pendleton thought he was going to have a hand-holding stroll around the harbour, a more friendly than friendly holiday with her, did he have another think coming!

But, good manners prevailing, rather than snatch her hand out of his and so draw the attention of their hosts to the fact that there was a hint of animosity in their camp, Elyss opted to make Saul release her hand by another method.

'What gives, Pendleton?' Elyss asked in a short undertone. 'Afraid of getting lost?'

His reaction was unexpected—he grinned. 'Oh, Elyss Harvey,' he murmured, and while she was again thinking in angry terms, he raised the hand he held to his lips—and kissed it!

He had released her hand before she could snatch it back, and she was left mid-way between wanting to hit him and—most odd of all—wanting to grin herself.

She supposed her lips must have twitched a little, for all her stern attempt not to smile, because Saul coaxed, 'Go on, you're on holiday.' Her lips involuntarily twitched again, and she turned her head away.

Elyss had seen nothing of their luggage since it had been spirited away at the airport. She did not lay eyes on it again until they disembarked from the motor launch that had brought them to the island of Kafros. They left the launch and transferred to a four-wheeled drive vehicle that Cato, who helped look after the villa, had brought to meet them.

The island, Elyss considered, was as idyllic as Saul had made it sound. With clear blue skies overhead and blissful warmth—the May chill of England left behind—Kafros's green-forested hills were a backing cloth to the sea. Above all, it was peaceful. What better spot in which to unwind?

Most oddly, just then she began to wonder how long

it had been since Saul had had chance to relax, to take a holiday, to unwind? He must work terribly hard. He deserved a break from... Good grief! She caught herself up short. She must be going soft in the head. To hear Louise tell it, he played every bit as hard as he worked.

It took them around a half an hour to reach the villa, and that too was beautiful. White-walled, red-roofed— and large. With its many balconied rooms, Elyss felt it was more like a small hotel. And, luxury of luxuries, as well as having the sea almost at the door, it also had its own swimming pool.

The housekeeper, Ismena, dressed all in black but with a sunny smile, was waiting in the hall as they went in. She spoke little English but Cato, her husband, who was bringing the remainder of their luggage, seemed to know more.

Elyss looked around the cool interior while some dis- cussion about rooms was going on, then Saul turned to her. 'I'll show you upstairs, Elyss,' he offered.

She went to pick up her suitcase. Saul was there be- fore her. He picked up his own as well. She might have argued but guessed she'd be wasting her time. Let him be the one to have a hernia.

Everywhere in the villa seemed wonderfully cool, with the doors to all the rooms open for the moment to allow the air to circulate. Upstairs Saul led the way down a long corridor, turning into a room about halfway down on the right.

Elyss followed him in, her glance taking in the dark wood of the furniture and the double bed as she went through onto the balcony, hoping she had a view of the sea. She had!

She went delightedly back into the bedroom, only for alarm to go shooting through her when she saw that Saul had hefted his suitcase on the bed and was unstrapping it. He was unpacking! She took a hurried glance to the door. He had closed it behind them.

'No way!' she erupted, her tone heated, angry. She wasn't having this! She...

Saul looked up from his case, which was open on what *she* regarded as *her* bed. And, in that way he had of getting instantly on her wavelength, Elyss saw that at once he knew to what she was referring.

His lips quirked. Give her strength! One of these days... 'You mean—I'm sleeping on the floor?' He seemed surprised, yet, as his eyes roved over her angry expression, all at once very serious too.

'You can sleep where the devil you like as long as it's *outside* my door,' Elyss snapped furiously, and was glaring at him, ready for further battle, when suddenly she saw that even while he tried to keep his expression serious there was a light of laughter dancing in his eyes.

'Heartless wench!' he teased her, and then, extracting something from his case before snapping it shut, he said casually, 'Just in case you didn't think to bring one, I bought you a hat.'

So saying, he tossed a wide-brimmed fold-away cotton hat at her, and enjoying her shaken expression—if his own was anything to go by—he took his case and himself off; she had the room to herself.

Swine! Teasing, tormenting toad! Clever brute—how did he know she hadn't thought to bring a hat and that her fair skin easily burned? She started to unpack, unaware that she was smiling.

Elyss finished her unpacking, realising that it had never been in Saul's mind to sleep with her. Which was just as well for him because he wasn't going to. Though, strangely, she did not feel in the least awkward because she'd as good as accused him of having designs in that area. And that surprised her. She would have thought she would be mortified with embarrassment at so falsely accusing him. Then she realised that the teasing manner he had adopted was responsible for her lack of embarrassment.

Elyss quite unexpectedly found that she liked him! Saul knew that she had not wanted to come, and that given free choice and without that debt hanging over her there was no way she would be here, as sunny, tranquil and pleasant as it was. Yet, the way things were—and given he thought her a lippy shrew—he was being charming to her.

She showered in the adjoining bathroom and changed into shorts and a sleeveless T-shirt. Fancying a break on a recliner in the sunshine, she went and took a look over the balcony. Madeline and Roland were stretched out on loungers down by the poolside. Elyss changed her mind about going down there.

Somehow she didn't want to intrude. Was this how Saul felt? Was that why he had wanted her, little—well, five feet eight, actually—uncomplicated old her along? So that his hosts wouldn't think that something was amiss if he didn't spend every minute with them? Pictures of Saul with Madeline at that party, Madeline at Saul's flat, jumped into Elyss's head. She pushed them out again, weary of trying to sort out what had been going on, or, indeed, wondering if she could believe that nothing was. She wasn't going to think about it, she determined. Hang it; apart from spending some time in Devon, this was likely to be the only holiday she would get this year. She was, she suddenly decided, going to enjoy it.

Spying the hat Saul had given her, she snatched it up

from the bed and opted to find a side way out of the villa. Time to do a little exploring. But hardly had she discovered an exit that led to some splendid gardens than she met Saul, clad in shorts and sports shirt, coming in.

She had never been shy in her life. However, now she lowered her eyes for a confused moment. 'You've got nice toes,' she said, apropos of nothing, lost for anything clever to say and espying his sandal-clad feet.

She raised her eyes, feeling a fool and a tinge pink about her cheeks. She met his warm grey eyes head-on. Saul studied her face, and the confusion she was striving to overcome.

'You're lovely,' he said softly.

'I'm—er—going exploring,' she informed him.

'If I'm very good, can I come with you?'

She laughed. She had to. Saul stared at her, his eyes going from her eyes down to her laughing mouth, then they slid to the hat she carried in her hands.

Taking it from her, he positioned in on her head. She looked up again, her eyes for the moment unshaded by the wide brim as she gazed at him. 'Mmm, quite lovely,' he confirmed, and Elyss had the oddest notion that he was going to kiss her. Odder still, she knew that she would not mind if he did.

Simultaneously they took a step away from each other. 'Thank you—for the hat,' she said jerkily, and, as together they started to walk towards a garden path, felt a babble of words coming on. 'You didn't... Did you buy it yourself?'

'Shall we go this way? If we turn left at that olive tree, we'll eventually hit the beach,' he answered. She directed her feet the way he suggested, and thought she was going to have to wait for a proper answer about her hat. But then Saul informed her, 'I came across my PA displaying the spoils of a pre-holiday lunch-time shopping spree to one of her colleagues yesterday.'

'You never bought it off her?' Elyss exclaimed, aghast.

'She was rather attached to it—I doubt she'd have sold it to me. Even though I did tell her I knew a fair maid who would blister and burn if she didn't have it.'

Inwardly Elyss's heart danced. For no reason she suddenly felt good. 'So?' she queried.

'So I sent her out to get another one.'

'For me?'

'Especially for you,' he replied.

Elyss felt charmed by him. Was this how it happened? How women were swept off their feet by him? 'It's—um—a good fit,' she murmured, and gave her full attention back to her surroundings, noticing trees, shrubs, flowers, well watered lawns and how the path curved round and down towards the sea.

Saul Pendleton was heady stuff. She acknowledged that fact only then. They reached the beach, where she kicked her sandals off and headed towards the water. She needed some space. Grief, all he'd done was to kiss her once on the cheek, to briefly hold her hand after lunch today—and she was going to pieces.

What was worse was the thought of him joining her, as the water lapped over her toes and she started to paddle, but just as if he'd discerned that she was in need of some privacy, he went and took his ease in the shade of an overhanging rock and left her to have all the space she needed.

He, she realised, knew far too much about women. So, what was she going to do about it? Well, for sure she wasn't going to sit and simper at him! Heaven forbid! She supposed he might have already witnessed he had the power to confuse her. Well, that was going to stop.

She left the water and walked casually back across the sand. Then, still some distance away from him, and certain she had a good fifty yards' start, she yelled, 'Come on, Pendleton,' across the sand. 'I'll race you back!' she didn't wait to see if he was joining in, but hared off towards the villa.

The incline down to the sea seemed far more steep on the return trip than she remembered it. She had always been able to sprint, though it had been some while since she'd breasted a race tape. But then it must have been even longer since Saul had taken part in a school sports day.

He caught her up as she rounded the olive tree—and he'd stopped to pick up her sandals *en route*! By the time she reached the villa Saul was leaning nonchalantly against the wall, looking as though he'd been there all day.

'What kept you?' he drawled.

She was gasping for breath and leant against the wall next to him. 'You cheated!' she accused, totally unfairly, and laughed because of her unfairness.

'For that, I shall claim my reward,' Saul declared, his tone light as he looked at her merry face.

He took her by the shoulders. Oh, Lord, he was going to kiss her—where was her resistance? Just the feel of his hands, warm on the skin of her shoulders where the cotton material of her T-shirt didn't cover her, was making her dizzy.

'If you could hurry up and get it over with—I think I'll need to shower again before dinner.'

'Oh, sweetheart, I never do this sort of a thing in a hurry,' Saul drawled. Why wasn't he out of breath? She was panting like an express train. His head started to come nearer. She swallowed, and closed her eyes.

She felt his body against her, part of him against her rising and falling chest. Then, when she fully expected him to kiss her mouth, she felt the warm, intimate touch of his lips against the side of her neck. Her legs went like water.

Suddenly it was over. He was pulling back. 'There just isn't room for two of us under that hat,' he remarked. He could have been coolly asking her something like, Have you any idea what time it is? he seemed so totally unaffected.

Elyss sought for something bright to return. 'What are the eating arrangements, by the way?' she asked, food the last thing on her mind as, casually, testing the strength of her legs, she peeled herself away from the wall.

'We'll eat in about half an hour,' Saul answered, opening the door for her. 'Just time for that shower.'

They went up the stairs together, Saul handing her sandals over at her bedroom door. 'See you,' Elyss said over her shoulder, and went into her room and closed the door. My stars, what a man! Suave, sophisticated, charming—yet quite at home accepting her challenge to belt back to base and see who could get there first.

She touched a sensitive hand to her neck where his lips had touched.

Elyss had herself back together again by the time she was showered and dressed in a lightweight dress of palest orange. She guessed that dinner at this holiday villa would be informal. And it was.

The other three were already downstairs when she went into the large, pleasantly furnished sitting room.

'What would you like to drink, Elyss?' her host smiled as she joined them.

'Something long and thirst-quenching, please,' she answered, and somehow seemed to have gravitated near to where Saul was standing. She went to move away, then felt his hand gently restraining her.

'Come and sit over here,' Saul invited.

She glanced to where Madeline was already seated, and moved with Saul to a nearby sofa.

'It's lovely here, tranquil,' Elyss commented, thanking Roland for the ice-cold drink he handed her.

'We like it,' he replied, and conversation became general and easy, until Ismena came to indicate that dinner was ready.

Conversation over dinner was equally as relaxed, with Elyss gaining the impression that Madeline preferred to do nothing but laze around when she was on holiday. Elyss neither liked nor disliked Madeline, but did not want to spend the whole day tomorrow down by the pool searching to find safe topics of conversation that didn't touch upon Saul Pendleton until he and Roland returned. Who knew, the men might not finish their business on the mainland until early evening?

'I think perhaps I might do a little exploring tomorrow!' she mentioned to Roland after he had just finished saying how safe the island was, and how pretty.

'Don't forget to wear your hat!' This from Saul, sitting next to her.

For absolutely no reason—other than perhaps because everyone seemed to be looking at her—Elyss felt herself go more than a tinge pink about the ears. So much so that she found herself explaining, 'Saul bought me a hat.' Oh, Lord—sophisticated!

She was just about wanting to curl up and die at how

gauche she sounded when Saul, with his warm grey-eyed look on her, remarked, 'And very lovely you look in it too.'

She glanced at him, and as his glance held hers she felt strangely unable to look away. Oh, grief, his look, that comment, everything seemed far more intimate than it was. 'You're only saying that because I let you beat me when we ran back...' Her voice tailed off. She wanted to groan. Gauche! Keep your mouth shut. Don't say another word!

Tearing her gaze away from Saul, she caught Roland looking at her with kindly regard. It was as if it pleased him that she and Saul had an easy, relaxed, untroubled relationship.

She concentrated her attention on her fruit salad. She had no idea how Madeline was taking any of it. Nor would she look. For some reason—and, exhausted, Elyss had done with trying to think out the whys and the hows of it—Saul wanted her there as his woman-friend. Well, she guessed that between her telling everyone that he had bought her a hat, and also that they were in the habit of having sprinting contests, she had just established that a friend she was.

Elyss supposed she must be grateful to Saul because, just as if he had discerned that she felt a mite discomforted, he had begun a discussion of other matters. So that, by the time they were drinking coffee, she was well on the way to forgetting that she had ever felt any discomfiture at all.

They had dawdled pleasantly over dinner, but by the end of it Elyss was aware that Saul and Roland needed a half-hour or so in Roland's study to go over their work tomorrow.

Which gave her the ideal opportunity to make herself

scarce once the meal was over. She felt peculiar somehow. Not ill. More on edge. As if there was something
happening in her life over which she had no control. She
did not like the feeling. It made her restless.

'I think I'll have an early night—if no one minds,'
she said generally as they left the table. She saw
Madeline give her a swift look.

Elyss had said her goodnights and was halfway up the
stairs to her room when, only then, she realised how her
wish to have an early night could be misinterpreted. She
was here as Saul's woman-friend.

Oh, heck! Was 'woman-friend' meant to convey that
she was having an affair with him? So, okay, they had
been allocated separate bedrooms—but in the world that
Saul, Roland and Madeline lived in that signified nothing, except when it came to actual sleeping: in a warm
climate one preferred to sleep alone.

But, hang on a minute. Wasn't Madeline herself having an affair with...? Elyss deliberately stopped her
thoughts right there. She was not, not, *not* going all over
that again. She wasn't sleepy; she wasn't going to bed
yet. Once in her room, she got out a book and, settling
in an easy chair, began to read.

Yet somehow even her favourite author of the moment failed to hold her interest. She read three pages—
and had to read the third page again because her
thoughts kept drifting.

She didn't want to sleep with Saul, for goodness'
sake! Nor did he want her to; that had been established
before coming here, when she'd told him point-blank
that she was not going to. 'When did I ask?' he had
enquired. Swine. Not that it really niggled her in any
way, shape or form. Huh! Nor did it bother her in the
slightest that, only that afternoon, even when he called

her 'Heartless wench', it was obvious that it had never been in Saul's mind to sleep with her.

Heavens above—when had she got onto this track? She did not, not, *not* care one tiny remotest bit that Saul Pendleton did not fancy her. Grief, there were far more important things in life than... Noises, someone coming up the stairs, caused her to stop her thoughts right there, and to listen.

No voices, just one set of footsteps—coming her way. She put her book down. Those footsteps halted outside her door. She knew who it was—she just did. He knocked. Well, things *were* looking up! Saul had actually knocked!

Elyss went to answer it; before this, regardless of in what state of *deshabille* she might be in, he would have walked in without bothering to knock.

She opened the door. It *was* Saul. Her heart fluttered. 'I'm all out of bedtime stories,' she told him sharply— just in case she'd got it wrong and this was a lead-up to something her mother had warned her about.

Elyss would have closed the door then, but, without so much as a by-your-leave—much more in keeping— Saul walked into her room and closed the door. She opened her mouth and was ready to blast him when suddenly, as he stared at her explosive expression, he smiled. Her heart fluttered in that crazy, nonsensical way again. Oddly, she forgot what it was she'd wanted to say.

'Not in bed yet?' he enquired of her still fully dressed self.

'Forgive me—I didn't know you were going to call,' she acidly found from somewhere.

He stared at her. She knew from the laughter in his eyes that she had amused him. 'Oh, Elyss Harvey, you're different, most definitely different. But put your hackles down.' The laughter in his eyes was replaced by a gentle kind of warmth, 'I merely looked in to say that Roland and I will be off very early in the morning, long before you're out of bed. I want you to enjoy your day.'

'Without you? I'll try.'

His lips twitched. 'You're one fantastic lady.'

'You're still not getting into my bed.' He ran a finger lightly down her nose, and suddenly that touch of his skin on hers seemed to get to her. She wanted to add something flippant, but nothing came, and, in any case, her throat seemed all at once so dry she doubted that she could have said another word had she attempted it.

'I don't know what time we'll be back,' he stated, and quite unexpectedly it dawned on her that Saul was far more sensitive than she had realised.

'I'll be all right,' she managed, albeit a little huskily. For surely that was why he must have thought to look in—to reassure her, should she in any way be in need of reassurance. 'If you're not back by dark—shall I put the cat out?' she asked lightly.

'You'll do,' Saul said softly, and taking her—unresisting—by the shoulders, he gently laid his mouth against her own. Then he stepped back. She stared at him, desperately needing to say something, but there were no words there. His kiss had in no way been meant to seduce—she knew that, understood that—but nevertheless she felt seduced by it. 'Goodnight,' he said.

''Night,' she answered, and was glad when he went. Just one tiny gentle kiss, and she was floundering. Heaven help her if ever he kissed her for real!

CHAPTER SIX

SAUL'S gentle kiss of the previous evening was much on Elyss's mind when she took herself off on a leisurely walk the next morning. He hadn't meant anything by it, of course. She supposed, in the circles in which he moved, people were always kissing each other—though why she should suppose that, she wasn't terribly sure at all.

In fact, she realised, she wasn't very sure of anything very much any more. She owned to the truth that she was growing more and more attracted to Saul—even though she didn't want to be attracted to him. Saul, when he wasn't being bossy and ordering her around, had rather a nice way about him.

As he had intimated, he and Roland were up and away long before the rest of the household stirred. Elyss breakfasted alone and, Madeline not having surfaced yet, she signed to Ismena that she was going for a walk.

For all that her walk was most pleasant, however, it seemed to Elyss to be a very long morning. She returned to the villa around two—and felt her heart start to pump energetically. Purely from her exertions, she was certain—though it was odd how her heartbeat calmed down to a dull, steady plod when she discovered that Saul, and Roland, of course, were not back yet.

Elyss had arrived at the villa just as Madeline, declaring it was too hot to sit outside—even in the shade—had decided that she was going to have a rest on her bed. 'I've asked Ismena to put some sandwiches in your room—but if you prefer something cooked…'

'Sandwiches will be fine.' Elyss thanked her hostess and went up the stairs with Madeline, conversing about the safe topic of her walk as they went.

By the time Elyss had showered away the perspiration of her morning's energies and returned to her room, she found that Ismena had been in with a tray of refreshments.

It was hot. Elyss lay on top of her bed in her cotton robe and, after a thirst-quenching drink of orange juice and a few sandwiches, she reached for her book.

She had no idea of when she went to sleep, and was only aware that she had drifted off when she heard the sound of male voices. They were back!

Suddenly, she was wide awake. She checked her watch on the table beside her. Six-twenty. How long had she been asleep, for goodness' sake? She heard the closing of two doors, and was all at once restless. What if Saul should come looking for her? Then she realised that he had only been gone for a few hours, and she had missed him, and she felt thoroughly confused.

In one enormous hurry she yanked her swimsuit from a drawer, quickly got into it, and, pausing only to collect a towel, she went swiftly and silently from her room.

Having exited by the side door, she was on that part of the beach she had been to yesterday with Saul before she gave herself chance to wonder what the dickens she was panicking about. Why would she think Saul would come looking for her?

It's the sun, she decided. I'm not used to it. Dropping her towel down on the sand as she went, Elyss strolled to the water's edge. She had forgotten her hat—oh, Saul!

What was the matter with her? She had forgotten her sunglasses too!

Lost in thought, she started to paddle along the shore-line. Still feeling unsettled, she turned about with some vague notion of paddling for a while. A movement to her right caught her eye. She stopped dead, her heart racing as Saul, clad in swimming shorts, saw her, and came over straight away.

'You're back,' she said in greeting—oh, brilliant—what next obvious observation would she make?

'Had a good day?' Saul asked, his glance skimming over her long-legged form clad in her one-piece bathing suit.

'Great!' she exclaimed, with no memory just then of any of it. 'Things go well for you?' she asked, the sight of his broad, naked, manly chest doing everything to aid her confusion. She turned from him and started to wade deeper into the sea.

'Pretty much as expected,' he replied, wading in be-side her. 'You swim?'

'I'll teach you if you like.'

'Did I say you were lippy?'

'It's the effect you have on me,' she tossed at him, and, in deep enough, she took a dive under the water.

For how long they swam under and on top of the water, Elyss had no idea. Nor did she particularly care. All she knew just then was that she was the happiest she had ever been.

They had both been swimming underwater, and sur-faced about a yard from each other at the same time. Her breath caught; he looked so superb, water glistening on his hair and his chest, where dark hair clung wetly; he was all chest, arm and shoulder muscles.

Elyss had no idea what she looked like, but as Saul

stared at her blonde hair she raised her hand and self-consciously raked her hair back from her face.

He was still staring at her when her feeling of self-consciousness started to get the better of her. She was just about to dive beneath the water again, when Saul seemed to read what she was about to do.

'Time to come out, little mermaid,' he called a halt to the wonderful time she had been having—and she resented it.

'I'll come out when I'm ready!' Elyss erupted. Bossy brute. She didn't want to come out yet. She didn't want *him* to come out yet. She took a defiant dive beneath the water—and didn't get two yards before he caught her and hauled her up.

She came up squealing, wriggling—and laughing. She couldn't help it. He had her in a firm grip when, as if she weighed nothing, he shot her high out of the water, holding her there aloft by her waist. She looked down at his devil-may-care face, her own expression laughter-filled.

'Let me down!' she begged, her hands on his shoulders—and had her wish when, holding onto her so she should not swim away, Saul gradually let her down.

Her legs came into contact with his body, her body came into contact with his body and there seemed to be something happening which again she could not control. Her arms went round him, clutching at him as if in need of some sort of support.

She looked at him, saw that he seemed stunned too. 'Saul.' She said his name. She needed some kind of help here.

'Elyss,' he murmured, though she didn't suppose he was in need of any sort of help, and held her close up against him.

It seemed natural then that, locked in each other's arms as they were, they should kiss. Their lips met, and it was wonderful for Elyss. Her head swam, she clung onto him, never wanting his kiss to end.

But it did end. Not hurriedly, not in a rush, but gently. Saul placed a hand to one side of her face, and she stared at him. She wasn't embarrassed, she discovered, but felt highly emotional.

Which was perhaps why she took her eyes from him and looked over his shoulder. And abruptly—she froze. She had been so enraptured she'd had no idea which way she had been facing.

She discovered she was looking at the beach which not so long ago she and Saul had had to themselves. But no longer. For there, in the shade of the overhanging rock where Saul had taken his ease yesterday, Madeline Scott now stood. She, too, was swimsuit-clad, and she was standing staring at them as they embraced, and must have witnessed that kiss.

'Let go of me!' Elyss cried in no uncertain terms.

'My dear, there's nothing...'

My dear! She'd *kill* him! 'Your girlfriend's watching!' Elyss exploded, and, feeling sick inside, when he relaxed his hold to turn and glance to the beach, Elyss pushed away from him and went rocketing back to the villa.

She stayed under the shower for an age. She wouldn't cry, she wouldn't. She washed the sea from her hair, the salt from her body, and was determined not to cry. Why would she cry? That two-timing rat of a man!

Had he known Madeline was there watching them? Had he coldly, calculatingly kissed her because he had fallen out with Madeline over something? The swine, the absolute monster. Had he kissed her in cold blood, purely because he'd had some spat with Madeline and was out to show her that there were other fish in the sea? Oh, it was unbearable!

As it was just as unbearable when she stepped out of the shower to find that she had left her bath towel down on the beach—she doubted that this time Saul had carried her belongings back to the villa for her.

Damn Saul; she hoped the jellyfish got him—preferably a Portuguese man-of-war. She'd go down to the beach for the towel later. Meantime... Elyss dabbed at herself with a remaining, smaller towel and then, remembering seeing some spare towels on some shelves in the side of the wardrobe, she wrapped her hair in the one towel, and left the bathroom to go in search.

She was four steps into her room when a small sound of utter fright escaped her. For, leaning against the wall, clearly aware that she would soon appear from the bathroom—though with no idea that she would appear stark naked—was Saul.

In that split second when his glance fleetingly caught her pink-tipped breasts and the rest of her long-legged nakedness she was in panic and already in flight. But Saul must have acted simultaneously—and like lightning—because before she could hit the bathroom again, and almost as if suspecting that once in there she might never come out again, Saul had the towel he had brought with him wrapped around her.

'Shh...' he soothed. 'I'm not going to harm you.'

'That's true!' she hissed, though she wasn't promising the same if he ever let her go.

He moved with her to the bed, picking up the cotton robe reposing at the foot of it. 'Put your arms into this,' he instructed and, modesty preserved, only when she was neatly wrapped and the robe belt tied, did he remove the towel. Heavens above, was there no end to his accomplishments?

'You've done that before!' she accused aggressively, stepping away from him and wishing he would clear off. She needed to get herself together. What chance was there with him here? There she was with her head turbanned in a towel and a thin robe clinging to her body. He, she observed, was showered and now dressed in shirt and trousers.

'Not that I recall,' Saul replied evenly, his glance steady on her flushed face.

He was calm; she was agitated and she wanted him gone. 'Does your lady-love know you're here?' she challenged—perhaps being reminded of Madeline would make him go.

'My lady-love?' he echoed—and she could have slaughtered him.

'Don't come that butter-wouldn't-melt innocence with me!' Elyss raged. Oh, to be dressed with a bit more dignity. 'I object, most strongly, to being used as a cover for the love affair you're having with—'

'Don't be—'

'And neither do I take kindly to being—b-being k-kissed only for the benefit of an audience which—'

'An audience?' he queried, cutting in again, this man whom she well knew was the sharpest man, the quickest on the uptake, that she had ever met. 'Ah, Elyss,' he said softly, and took a step closer, and added succinctly, 'There's no audience here now.'

She took a few rapid backing paces from him. 'You keep away from me!' she charged, her voice rising.

He halted at once. 'I'm sorry,' he apologised. 'I didn't mean to alarm you—perhaps a brief kiss, no more.'

'Save your brief kisses—and otherwise—for her!'

Elyss flew, and might have said more, only, from the look on Saul's face, she had an idea that something pretty astonishing had just presented itself to him.

'You're—jealous!' he exclaimed.

'You're nuts!' she retaliated, and charged on lest his crazy notion should take root with him. 'I'm honest, that's all—and you're not!' Oh, he didn't like that, did he? She saw his brow come down, but did not care. At least she'd got him away from that one very delicate subject. 'And—and I find it offensive,' she ploughed on, 'that-th—'

'You're honest!' Saul cut in; if there was any offence to be taken here, it was he who was going to take it, after having his honesty questioned. 'No doubt law abiding too!' He took a step nearer. 'You wouldn't dream of driving around without motor insurance or...'

'You louse!' she flew, outraged. Her aggressiveness was out looking for a target, too, as she took a step nearer to take a swing at him. 'You...' Her hand arced through the air.

It didn't make contact. Not with his face as she'd intended, anyway, because Saul, with his stunningly fast reactions, caught a firm hold of her wrist. Frustrated beyond bearing that the swipe that had been on its way to him almost from the first moment she had met him had come to nought, Elyss gave him a gigantic shove. He still had a hold of her wrist—but she was the one who went off balance first. She landed on the bed—Saul landed with her. They landed with their backs on the mattress.

She didn't know whether she was winded or what. Or, how Saul was. For all was totally still, totally silent— for about five seconds. Then all at once that stillness, that silence was broken.

Saul's body beside her moved—and he laughed. Her lips twitched. It wasn't funny! Desperately she tried to suppress her inner sense of the ridiculous—but could not. Flat on her back, Saul's right hand still somehow manacled to her wrist—and whether it was a release from tension or just her sense of humour rising up to meet his, she had no idea—laughter bubbled up inside her and refused to be pushed down again. Her body shook—she laughed.

Saul rolled onto his side, letting go of her wrist as he propped himself up on one elbow and looked down at her. 'You, Elyss Harvey, are something else again,' he murmured.

'I know,' she lied—something *was* happening to her and she knew *nothing*.

'Are you going to forgive me for not letting you fracture my jaw?'

'Don't I always?' she smiled.

His wonderful mouth curved, but, on a shaky kind of groan, he owned 'I want, quite desperately, to kiss you, Elyss Harvey.'

'Saul Pendleton, I don't think you should,' she lied again.

His left hand came up, his forefinger stroking down the side of her face. Her spine went like water. 'Not even a very tiny kiss?'

'I think you're seducing me.'

'I'm feeling much the same way,' he breathed. He bent his head and their lips met.

'I—I th-think you should go,' the liar inside Elyss tried to be heard when, gently, Saul broke their spell-binding kiss.

'I'm sure you're right,' he answered, and moved,

though only far enough to place his left arm around her. 'Please say something to make me go,' he pleaded.

She almost said, I love you. 'I...' she began, and changed it to, 'Is this really happening to me?'

'You're not—worried?' he asked gently.

She shook her head, denying herself the need to swallow. Why would she be worried? She was near naked, lying on a bed with a man whom she urgently wished would kiss her again. 'No, I'm not worried,' she answered huskily—and had her urgent wish granted when Saul lowered his head again.

His lips met hers on a sigh of a kiss. He raised his head and looked into her trusting rich blue eyes. And, as if his need to kiss her was quite desperate, he once more claimed her lips.

He moved closer. Elyss pressed herself to him. She felt the heat of him through her thin robe. Saul lay half over her, his kisses seeming to draw on her very soul.

He kissed her neck; she kissed his neck—he had a lot to teach her. He kissed the side of her face. She kissed the side of his face. He looked down at her.

'You're wonderful,' he breathed.

'You're a wonderful teacher,' she whispered shyly.

'Ready for the big girls' class?' he queried, and she laughed, a light joyous, wanting laugh.

'I think so,' she accepted—when she knew full well she could have refused and it would have ended right there.

'Stop me—if there's anything you don't understand,' he teased softly.

She wanted him to kiss her, and he did. More than that, he traced mind-bending tender kisses all the way down her throat. He looked up and at her trusting gaze, seemed unable to resist raising his head and placing a whisper of a kiss on her eyelids before claiming her lips unhurriedly and tenderly.

In fact all his actions seemed relaxed, as he held her close and caressed her through her thin robe. Most unhurriedly of all, his hands caressed their way to her breasts.

Elyss clutched onto him. 'All right?' he questioned. She nodded. She was too full to speak, and did not wish to do so when his kisses began to deepen and the hands that had been on the outside of her robe searched with a sureness inside it.

She felt the warmth of him as his sensitive fingers and palms caressed and moulded the silken skin of her breasts. And a fire burned out of control in her for him when, lowering his head, he parted her robe and tenderly kissed the hardened pink tip of each breast in turn.

'You're beautiful,' he breathed, and Elyss was so full of desire for him she didn't even acknowledge that there was no turning back now. She just instinctively knew that there wasn't.

Well, not from her point of view anyhow. Nor, she thought, from his. But they had both reckoned without outside intervention. For just as Saul had claimed her mouth again, and was enchantingly moulding and caressing her right breast, they both heard someone come knocking on the door.

Elyss was too far gone for comprehension. But, for the first time since Saul had begun to make love to her, she felt a hint of panic. The knocking came again—and suddenly it dawned on her that anyone might come in!

'Saul!' she cried in alarm.

He seemed to have come down to earth too. Swiftly he covered her breasts with the material of her robe, and in the next second was off the bed and over at the door.

Elyss leapt from the bed as well, making a dive for the bathroom and hoping against hope that as Saul opened the door, Ismena would come into her room for something and she would not notice the state of the rucked-up bedcover.

Elyss still had the bathroom door open, her escape all but complete, when she realised that she had got it wrong. It wasn't Ismena at all—but Madeline Scott!

'Oh, Saul—I've looked everywhere for you. I had to see you. We just have to talk!' she heard Madeline cry.

What Saul answered Elyss didn't hear, but as he closed the door of her bedroom firmly after him so a dry sob racked her. That sound of the door closing had a wealth of significance to it, as far as she was concerned.

Quite clearly, by closing that door, Saul Pendleton had said that whatever had gone on between them less than a couple of minutes ago—forget it. Madeline Scott was his first and only priority.

Elyss did not want to go down to dinner that night. She wasn't in the least hungry, and felt sick at heart. How could he? How could she?

She remembered the way she had responded to his kisses. The way she had wanted him to make complete love to her. The certainty she'd felt that she would not have drawn back had it got that far. And she could only wonder—had that wanton woman been her?

She had known from the night of the Scotts' party that Saul was involved with his good friend's wife. Oh, Elyss—where is your pride? You knew he was having an affair, and yet...

Pride hadn't come into it, though, had it? Saul only had to make her laugh—and he could do that seemingly without even saying a word—and she was putty in his hands.

Now she knew why she had initially backed away from him when he'd made some reference to there not being an audience now. Subconsciously she must have known that once he kissed her she would not be able to resist him.

Damn him, damn him to hell, she fumed, starting to grow angry. Saul had charmed her into liking him—and she hadn't seen the danger coming. She had fallen in love with him. Join the queue!

And why was he being charming to her? Because he wanted Roland Scott—the man he held in high regard—to believe that there was something between them, and therefore he could not possibly be interested in Roland's wife.

Louse! Double-dyed and vermin-infested; no, misbegotten lecher more aptly described him! And what of Roland's wife? No doubt she and Saul were busy handholding—that was a mild term for it!—right at this very moment.

Elyss reckoned her humiliation was complete when it suddenly came to her that Saul had in all likelihood explained to Madeline why he was toting Elyss Harvey along to parties and Greek holidays. She was his—their—cover, for their diabolical affair behind Roland Scott's back.

Elyss doubly did not want to go down to dinner. But she had shown a distinct lack of pride once already today.

It was pride alone that made her dress with care in a dress of turquoise silk. She wore a minimum amount of make-up, but brushed her hair till it crackled with life and energy and shone beautifully about her head.

She had not the smallest idea of what she was going to say to Saul when she saw him—but let him try to make her laugh tonight—he'd be on a hiding to nothing! As for Madeline—Elyss decided, for Roland's sake, that she was going to be pleasant to his wife even if it did hurt like hell.

On entering the sitting room, however, she discovered that, while her mouth forced a smile in Saul's general direction and her eyes smiled genuinely at Roland, Madeline was not well and would not be joining them.

'I'm sorry—nothing serious, I hope?' Elyss asked Roland, who was looking a little concerned.

'I don't think so—oddly, she seems more homesick than anything else.'

Elyss didn't believe Madeline was homesick for a moment. Though she owned to feeling a little cheered. If Madeline wanted to go home then she could only conclude that her little love-idyll with Saul wasn't working out as planned. What a shame!

Home! Suddenly Elyss saw a way of ending this farce. 'Actually, I was so excited when Saul invited me to join you—' she ignored Saul's expression '—that I clean forgot about my father's birthday—and that I promised to go down to Devon to see him at the weekend.'

'You wouldn't mind flying back tomorrow?' To her mind Roland was already starting to sound much relieved.

'I'd feel better not breaking my promise,' she owned. It was Saul Pendleton's fault—she hadn't been a liar until she had met him!

'We could always come back another time,' Roland suggested.

'I'd like that,' she replied, and it was half true, for

Kafros was a beautiful island—but... She couldn't finish, not if she didn't want to break down in tears.

They did not linger over-long at dinner. Elyss was aware of Saul's glance on her from time to time but he wasn't saying very much. She rather amazed herself, given that she addressed a point about six inches above his head, that she was able to say anything to him at all. Pride, she realised, was making up for its dastardly absence before.

She waited only to finish the last of her coffee before turning to her host. 'Would you mind if I dashed off and got on with my packing?'

'Not at all,' Roland excused her. 'I'll get on the phone and arrange a fairly early start.'

'I'll say goodnight, then.'

'You're not coming down again?' Saul asked, his tone even.

'There speaks a man who knows very little about women's packing,' she smiled at Roland and, holding back on the urge to give Saul Pendleton a clout on the ear as she passed, she went up to her room—where she abruptly sagged like some rag doll.

'You're not coming down again?' he'd asked. As if he wanted to see her! Hmpf! As if she wanted to see him. Oh, darn it, of course she wanted to see him.

They landed in England to weather that had improved only slightly in their absence. But the weather was the least of Elyss's worries. 'Do you mind if I hare off now?' she said brightly to anyone who might be interested, and, while three pairs of eyes concentrated on her, she made a pretence of checking her watch. 'If I go now I'll be in good time to catch the Plymouth train from Paddington.'

'I'll drive you to the station,' Saul volunteered. Trust him! She'd got no intention of going anywhere near a station—and rather thought he knew it.

'We're going that way, aren't we, darling?' Madeline had said barely anything the entire journey home—Elyss wished she had left it that way. 'You don't want to take Saul miles out of his way. We'll take you to the station.'

Of the two, and it seemed she was going to end up with either Saul or Roland driving her, Elyss thought she preferred the option of the Scotts—even if she did not want to go to Paddington.

'Thank you,' she accepted—what else!

They parted from Saul in the car park. Elyss had been hoping to get into the car without having to say another word to him. He caught hold of her arm. 'I'll ring you,' he promised, though for whose benefit she couldn't tell.

'I'll be back Monday,' said she who wasn't going anywhere—save maybe a taxi ride from Paddington railway station to her flat.

'My regards to your parents,' he added smoothly, every bit as if they were all well acquainted, and before she could stop him he bent and kissed her cheek.

Her skin tingled all the way to Paddington. Pig, swine, brute, she fumed, near to tears again and hating him. 'I'll ring you'—she'd never hear from him again. He knew it, she knew it—and in all probability Madeline Scott knew it too.

Elyss did not expect Madeline to get out of the car when Roland pulled up at the station terminus, so she said her thank-yous and goodbyes from there, while Roland was busy getting out her case.

'Thank you, Roland,' Elyss smiled at him. 'Your villa is in a beautiful place.'

'You haven't seen the last of it,' he beamed, and he kissed her cheek too.

Elyss stood and waved them goodbye and, when they were out of sight, she wheeled her case over the concourse—to the taxi rank.

'We didn't expect you till Sunday!' Nikki exclaimed when she got back to the flat. 'Oh, dear,' she added, the subject uppermost in her mind, 'You didn't fall out with your boyfriend?'

'I shall never see him again,' Elyss replied, a ready-made excuse for her early return there waiting. She knew now why Nikki so frequently burst into tears—being in love was hell! 'But I don't want to talk about it,' she added quickly, when all the signs were that Nikki was ready to offer a sympathetic shoulder.

'I'll make you some tea.' If only that would cure it!

Elyss was in her room unpacking when Victoria came home. Unable to delay going through to say hello some minutes later, Elyss guessed that Nikki had already informed Victoria that she was back from her trip and that boyfriends were a taboo subject.

'Glad you're back!' Victoria exclaimed, giving her a quick hug. 'We missed you.'

They seemed to chat about anything and everything after that—except men and holidays. 'Victoria and I are going to take a look at that new wine bar later on, do you fancy coming with us?' Nikki invited.

Elyss shook her head. 'I think I'll have an early night.'

Her mother rang soon after they had gone and Elyss felt quite dreadful when her parent asked if her flatmates had told her she had telephoned last evening. 'I said that there wasn't any message, but they may have mentioned my call.' A slight pause. 'They said you were out?'

'They didn't say you called,' Elyss replied, and, with

her thoughts darting back to yesterday, 'I was out swimming,' she explained; to explain what else she had been doing would give her mother heart failure.

She half expected her mother might ask who she had gone swimming with, and was no end relieved when her lovely parent went on blithely, 'You always were a brilliant swimmer.' Going on, her mother asked, 'You haven't forgotten your father's birthday a week tomorrow?'

'Nothing would keep me away,' Elyss promised.

Her father's birthday, and the fact that Saul Pendleton might believe she was in Devon celebrating it this weekend, was still in her mind a minute after her mother had rung off and the phone rang again.

As had happened a couple of times before, Elyss fully expected it to be her mother using the redial button with some matter she had previously rung to tell her expressly about but had forgotten as they chatted.

She picked up the phone. 'What did you forget?' she teased.

'Me—nothing!' replied the one and only voice that could make her heart pound. 'You—you forgot your way to Devon.' Tears stung her eyes. Saul, oh, Saul. She had thought she would never hear from him again. 'How *was* Devon?' he asked, when it didn't seem she was ever going to find her voice.

'So I lied,' she managed, striving hard to get herself all of one piece.

'Why?'

Her brain refused to function. She couldn't think of one single solitary answer. All she knew just then was that she was in love with him, that she was feeling all soft and helpless to hear him again, so wonderfully and unexpectedly. Then, out of nowhere, she started to recall that he wasn't feeling all soft about hearing her; he was having a very nice time with Madeline Scott, thank you very much—and suddenly the backbone Elyss needed had arrived.

She ignored his question. 'What do *you* want?' she demanded waspishly—and discovered her unpleasant tone affected him not one whit.

'Now, isn't that a fine greeting from my girlfriend?'

Her heart was racing, was 'girlfriend' a promotion from 'woman-friend', or the opposite? 'Get to the back of the queue, Pendleton!' she snapped. Though she never wanted him to ring off, to sever this thin connection, suddenly her pride took over. 'Look here, I'm busy.'

'You're with someone?' he rapped.

'That's nothing to do with you!' she retorted. Grief, it hadn't taken long for his tone to change, had it? Aggressive brute.

'Get rid of him!'

'Like blazes!' Bossy devil. 'I don't owe you...'

'What you owe me is the cost of repairs to my—'

Even as her breath caught in her throat she was cutting in. 'Oh, come on—' she began, but got no further.

And aggressiveness just wasn't in it when toughly he sliced her off. 'No, *you* come on. Our agreement was until Sunday—I'm not prepared to let you break that agreement.'

'But—we came home. We left Greece and...'

'And you still owe me two days.'

'Oh, for...'

'Which is why I've decided you can come to Norfolk with me tomorrow.'

'Norfolk!' Elyss gasped, starting to feel befuddled again.

'We've been invited to the country for the weekend.'

So it was to be a house party. But she was sensing something most diabolical in the woodshed. 'Count me out!' she snapped unhesitatingly. Silence. 'I'm not going!' she stated categorically. Silence still. Elyss mentally called him every vile name she could think of—but still, as if waiting for her to sort herself out, Saul remained silent. And sort herself out she did, as it all at once hit her that he once more wanted her around as cover for his clandestine affair. Of all the nerve! Like hell! 'I'm definitely not going if Madeline and Roland Scott are going to be there!' she erupted furiously. The cheating toad! If he thought...

'They won't be there,' Saul broke his silence to assure her calmly.

Her fury faltered—and dipped. But even if the Scotts wouldn't be there, she still didn't want to go. Saul had the power to turn her world upside down, to take away the control she had always had over her life—and, most of all, her weakness where he was concerned worried her. Had he cared anything about her, about any least little thing, it would have been different, but... Oh, for goodness' sake, stop dreaming, wake up; that he might care was never going to happen.

'When are *you* going?'

'*We* go tomorrow.'

Toad! 'And if I don't choose to come?' Pride cometh before a fall—she knew full well he had left her without choice.

'I'm sure you know the answer to that, sweet Elyss.'

The bailiffs! She loved him. And love was a treacherous monster—she wanted to see him, to be with him—even if that 'sweet Elyss' meant absolutely nothing. 'This will be it?' she questioned. 'If I come with you, then, afterwards, when I come back, my debt to you will be done?'

'After this, your debt will be settled,' Saul promised.

Elyss took a long, steadying breath, 'What time?' she asked.

'No need to rush. Shall we say, around eleven?'

Elyss switched off her phone. Was she mistaken, or had there been a smile in Saul's voice at the end of the call? Well, he would smile, wouldn't he? He ordered— she obeyed. His wish, it seemed was her command!

CHAPTER SEVEN

'HE—um—rang,' Elyss confessed to Nikki and Victoria on Saturday morning. 'My—er—friend...'

'You've made it up!' Nikki beamed, plainly delighted for her.

What could she say? Elyss would not have said anything at all had it not for the fact that she felt she needed to explain she would shortly be departing the flat with a weekend case. She didn't feel comfortable saying that she was going to see her parents. In any case her mother might well take it into her head to ring again.

'He's invited me to a house party. I'll—er—be away overnight.'

'Don't do anything I wouldn't,' Victoria quipped.

'*There's* licence for you!' Nikki chipped in—and they all laughed.

Elyss didn't feel much like laughing when a little after half past ten she started up her car and pointed it in the direction of Saul's home. She wanted to see him, of course she did. Quite desperately did she want to see him. To spend this weekend with him, even if there were going to be other people present, would be wonderful.

Stopping by a florists, Elyss purchased a bouquet to take to her hostess and got back into her car, feeling grateful that there would be other people there. She found her feelings for Saul quite overwhelming: she'd had no idea that being in love could be such a personality-changing experience. She had gone through the whole of her life never wanting to hit anybody, yet Saul, the man she was in love with, seemed adept at frequently making her want to box his ears!

Contrary to that, at other times she just wanted to be with him. Just to talk, to sit, to laugh with him. She wanted to hold him and to love him. And, one special time in particular, she had wanted to make love with him—and *that* had never happened before with any man.

Which made it especially important that other people should be around this weekend. Not that there would be any kissing—she'd take jolly good care of that. But, and she owned to feeling more than a little panicky about it, what she must do above all was to disguise, and not give away by word, look or deed, how very much she loved him.

Elyss reached Saul's apartment block and, suddenly very conscious that the weekend case she carried was a dead give-away that she was off somewhere for the weekend with Saul, endeavoured to be very grown-up about it when Bernard looked up as she went in.

'Ah, Miss Harvey. Mr Pendleton is expecting you. Would you like to go up?'

'If you could tell him I'm here. We're going to stay with friends—we're running a little late,' she excused; another little lie, but she felt better for it.

Bernard duly got busy with the phone, then, seeing she had her car keys dangling from the hand that held the bouquet, he enquired, 'Are you using your car, or would you like me to garage it for you?'

She handed over her car keys, and as Bernard disappeared out of the door heard sounds of the lift descending. Elyss turned her back to it, her heart racing. She needed a moment to get herself under control.

She heard the lift doors open and 'casually' turned. Oh, heavens, he was wonderful. Tall, straight, overnight bag in hand. She needed to say something, anything. 'Reporting for duty,' she said coolly, when Saul stepped out from the lift and, coming close, just stood looking down at her.

'Do I take it that you mean to obey *all* my orders?' he enquired.

She wanted to laugh. Why? He just had that effect on her. 'Forget it, Pendleton!' she snapped, and pushed the flowers at him.

'For me? You shouldn't have!'

Laughter bubbled up inside her. She managed a withering look. 'For our hostess!'

'Ah!' he replied, whatever that meant. 'I'd take your case, but I don't appear to have a free hand.'

Elyss preceded him out to the Ferrari and was startled to realise from its different coloured seats that it was a different car from the one in which Saul had driven her to the airport last Wednesday. He'd got his car back! She didn't think it politic to refer to it—the vehicle was immaculate, any repairs excellently carried out; excellent and costly, she rather thought.

She had, however, other concerns as they started on their way. A few minutes earlier she had wanted to laugh with him and already felt that her resolve was weakening. Not by word, look or deed! But why shouldn't she laugh again with him, be friends with him? Would it matter if she were? She could still guard her eyes, her tongue. And, good heavens, they were going to stay with friends of his. Courtesy to her hosts alone decreed that they should not know of any animosity between them. Good manners meant she should not in any way give their hosts reason to feel uncomfortable.

'So?' she questioned.

'I'm sure you're right,' he answered maddeningly.

'Would you like,' she ploughed on determinedly, 'to tell me a little about our hosts?'

'Of course, most remiss of me.' He checked the time. 'Would you like to stop for lunch?'

'When are we expected?'

'Any time,' Saul answered easily.

Elyss didn't think that good enough. She had no idea how many other people were expected. And it could be, of course, that their hosts had laid on a cold buffet for lunch but... 'We'd better eat now,' she decided—and Saul, as ever, took charge.

They pulled up at a very pleasant country hotel and were first in the dining room. She wasn't feeling very hungry, but ordered a chicken salad and looked about, wishing circumstances were different and that this was a proper date, a proper weekend, where Saul and she were guests of some friends of his as a real couple.

For goodness' sake! Ever wary of giving herself away, Elyss snapped out of it. It *wasn't* a proper date, for heaven's sake! Saul had merely brought her along because... She halted right there, suddenly astonished that her head had been so full of everything else she hadn't stopped to wonder—why her? Oh, she knew all about the money she owed him but—grief, he could have brought any one of a dozen... She halted again. She had been this route before.

'Why?' she challenged abruptly.

'Because it's there?' he suggested.

'Why me?' Elyss was not amused, and furious suddenly. 'If you're expecting me to cover for another of your sordid affairs, Pendleton, forget...'

'Sordid affairs!' he echoed, and all of a sudden seemed more pleased than angry. 'You're sure you're not a *tiny* bit jealous, Elyss?' he queried quietly.

She nearly died on the spot, and was within a centimetre of spluttering out a vehement protest. But somehow she managed to stay outwardly cool. 'There are egos, and then there are egos, Saul Pendleton. But I reckon yours, if you don't mind my saying, is the largest I've ever tripped over.'

He feigned to look disappointed. 'Damn—and there was me thinking I'd made another conquest.'

'Tough!' She looked at him. He smiled back—and she loved him so much. 'So why,' she made herself persist, when just then nothing else seemed to matter but that he should smile her way, 'why, out of all the other women you know—who don't owe you money,' she threw in, 'didn't you bring one of *them*?'

Saul looked at her steadily and, as her heart started to pound, she began to think he might give her a serious answer. But, while managing to maintain that steady-eyed look, 'Nobody dances quite like you,' he replied.

So they'd be dancing tonight? 'And?'

'And you've got a most attractive husky laugh.'

Somebody had mentioned that to her once before. 'And?'

'And never have I seen such rich, beautiful and astonishing big blue eyes.'

She was starting to melt. But mustn't. And, grief, she was sure she wasn't the only woman he knew with big blue eyes.

'You're a past master at this, aren't you?'

'What?'

And cut out the innocence too. 'The charm.'

'You're saying—I charm you?'

'Dream on!' she snapped waspishly, never likely to tell him that he had the power to turn her legs to jelly. 'Why me?' she insisted.

For several long serious moments Saul appeared to study her solemnly. His voice was serious too, when a second later he answered, 'It could be that I like you.'

'Huh!' she jibed—there was no other answer. He wasn't to know that her insides seemed to be somersaulting all over the place. Saul *liked* her! She was glad that, just then, her meal arrived. She gave it her full attention.

They were back on the road again when, rather belatedly admittedly—her head had turned to cotton wool just because Saul *liked* her?—she realised that he had never answered her question about the people they were going to stay with.

'Our hosts,' she immediately set about rectifying her tardiness.

'Yes?' Saul answered off-handedly—he seemed to be concentrating on his driving.

Far be it from her to distract him, but it wouldn't hurt him to tell her their names. 'Who are they?' she pressed.

He negotiated a bend. 'A couple by the names of Dorothea and Tudor,' he replied.

Of course she wanted to know more than that. Had he told them the name of the person he was bringing? Did she have to invent an answer other than—what was it he'd told Roland?—'Our paths seemed to collide' if asked how they had met? And who else would be there? Would she again stand at the top of some stairs to see him at the bottom with another female looking adoringly up at him!

Jealousy again began to bite, and Elyss was in the middle of having grave doubts about the wisdom of having said she would come—not that she'd had much choice in the matter—when Saul turned off the main road.

She guessed, as he steered the Ferrari up a narrow country lane, that they were near their destination. But, having expected that—since it was a *house* party they had been invited to—they would be staying in a house of some size, Elyss was not a little startled when Saul drove up to a very small cottage.

Of course, this couldn't be the place, she realised. More than four people in it and the walls would bulge! He must be stopping to ask for directions.

So why was he driving onto the car parking area? There was no garage. Saul braked. She sat. He took the key out of the ignition. Perhaps he automatically did that whenever he left his vehicle—be it only for a few minutes now, as he was going to ask for directions.

But he didn't move. That was save to turn and look at her. She wouldn't jump to conclusions, she wouldn't, she wouldn't. She was aware of his eyes on her face, aware of his scrutiny. Then his voice came. 'We're here,' he said.

She held down heated words, just as she held down her recently acquired urge to box his ears. 'This is our destination?' she enquired—nothing on God's earth was going to make her get out of this car.

'You'll love it,' he said. 'Come and take a look round.' He sounded enthusiastic—against her better judgement she got out of the Ferrari.

The cottage seemed even smaller than her parents' place. But it was quaint, with a pretty garden. In fact, it was quite enchanting. But by no manner of means was it a house. It was more, she would have said, a small weekend retreat. Ho! Ho! Rat-in-the-nostrils was the aroma of the day!

Her suspicions grew when, with not so much as a ring of the doorbell, or perhaps an apology or an—'Oh, dear—our hosts must be out.'—Saul inserted a key he'd brought with him into the door lock. The key fitted; the door opened instantly—what a surprise!

'Come in,' he invited.

If she had acted on instinct, Elyss would there and then have turned round and gone back to the car. But she made herself go in. When she went for his jugular, she wanted to be sure of her facts.

'You're sure Dorothea and Tudor won't mind?' she asked sweetly. Oh, for something solid and weighty to hit him with.

'Not a bit,' Saul replied. 'I'll explain about—'

'It's charming,' Elyss cut him off. Explain! What was there to explain? Quite plainly Madeline was busy elsewhere this weekend. Elyss Harvey—having been sampled and found moderately tasty in Greece—was the light relief. There wasn't much to see downstairs—a sitting room and kitchen. 'May I see upstairs?' she enquired politely.

The stairs, through a door, were wooden and narrow. There were two bedrooms and a tiny bathroom. The second bedroom was small, with room only for a single bed and a chest of drawers. Elyss turned to the main and large bedroom. Her suspicions were proved well founded—surprise, surprise, it housed a double bed!

'I thought you might like to have this room,' Saul, standing by her shoulder, commented.

He thought! Not their hostess—but *he* thought! 'Me?' She turned, her fury straining at the leash. 'Me, on my own?' she challenged. 'You're saying you're going to fit the length of you in that single bed while I spread myself out in the vast bed? How magnanimous of you.'

'You're upset!' Saul said quietly, adding soothingly, 'I didn't...'

'You're damn right I'm upset!' Elyss flew, in no mood to be soothed. 'I'm to sleep alone, am I—at this *house party*?'

'Now calm down. It isn't...'

'Calm down! How dare you?' she flew, her voice rising. 'What the hell do you think I am? Some—some cheap t-tart who can be bought for a few repairs to—'

'Enough!' Saul cut her off sharply; his soothing tone was soon gone she noted. 'That wasn't my purpose in bringing you here!'

'Like hell it wasn't. "We've been invited to the country for the weekend"!' she mimicked, toe to toe with him as he came close. He raised a hand as though to touch her arm. She knocked it furiously away. 'So where are the other guests—where?' She added icily, 'And where did you intend to put them?' Since clearly this was *his* weekend retreat—he'd probably invented Dorothea and Tudor—'You never invited anyone else did you?'

Perhaps she wouldn't have felt so bad if he'd had the decency to lie, to say he had invited other people, but that his guests were arriving later. But, none of it. 'No,' he answered. 'It was to be just you and me this weekend.'

And that was when she hit him. Bang! She was so dreadfully upset, blindingly angry, and churned up that this man she loved so well could use her so lightly, that Saul didn't have chance to catch hold of her wrist this time.

He did catch hold of her a split second later, though. 'You're becoming hysterical,' he stated tautly, his hands firm on her upper arms, holding them down.

'Is that a prelude to you hitting me back?' she fired. If it hadn't been for the fact that she feared losing her balance she'd have taken a mighty kick at him with her feet to make him let her go. But she didn't want him scraping her up off the bedroom carpet.

'Oh, Elyss, you little hot-head, I wouldn't hit you!' he denied.

'You've no doubt got more subtle ways to calm my hysteria!' she snapped.

But, oh, how she wished she had said nothing. Because Saul commented, 'Perhaps there is a way of shutting you up.' And, before she could begin to imagine what new-fangled method he had discerned of dealing with her, his mouth was over hers.

Shock kept her still for all of a second. And by that time Saul had gathered her to him and his arms were iron bands around her.

'No!' she gasped when, having successfully silenced her by the simple expedient of placing his mouth over hers, he finally broke his kiss.

'Are you going to behave while I try to explain?' he questioned.

'Keep your explanations, Pendle...' His mouth was back over hers before she could finish.

Elyss kicked out at him anyway, had the satisfaction of hearing him grunt as her aim found his shin. But she didn't fall, because he was holding her too tightly for that.

No, screamed her brain when, his mouth on hers once more, his kiss deepened. No! She fought for control as, gentling her now, Saul, while holding her firmly with one hand, tenderly stroked her back with the other.

She was losing control and knew it when those tender stroking movements became tender caressing movements. 'Saul!' she said on a gulp of breath when he broke his kiss.

'Don't be upset,' he murmured softly. 'I don't want you to be upset.'

'I'm...' She didn't know what she was, apart from perhaps glad when Saul, maybe in a further attempt to calm her down, gently kissed her again.

And, oh, she so wanted his kisses. Oh, how she wanted to be in his arms, needed to be in his arms. She stirred in his hold, a gesture of resistance—a futile gesture of resistance—because, whatever her head said, she did not want to hold back, she wanted to respond.

So tenderly did he kiss her that she just had to clutch onto him for support. Though quite when her clutching hands flattened out and became holding, hands that held him, she had no idea. All that she knew was she wanted him this close, needed him this close, needed to feel his warmth, was starved for his kisses.

And she was responding, holding, exchanging kiss for kiss. With a groan, Saul moulded her to him, sought her neck beneath her hair. A fire started to burn out of control in her for him.

'Saul.' She breathed his name, acquiescence to all he might wish in that small breathed sound.

'Elyss, little darling,' he murmured, his mouth on hers, and she was melting again. To be his little darling was what she desired more than anything on earth.

She pressed closer to him and he held her firmly, though somehow they seemed nearer to the bed than she remembered. But she wasn't remembering anything very much at all just then, when one of Saul's hands gently caressed the front of her linen dress.

She kissed him as he began to unbutton it, and had not the smallest protest to make when he slipped it from her shoulders. She started to tremble only when, while keeping a hold of her dress, he lowered it, so she should, if she wished, step out of it.

I love you, Saul, was all that was in her head when, her dress laid over a chair, a wisp of shyness came to visit. She moved closer to him, suddenly aware that she was clad only in her white lace slip and other scraps of underwear.

'You're wonderful,' Saul encouraged, and kissed her. Seemingly by mutual consent, their shoes disposed of without thought, they moved to lie with each other on the bed.

Elyss wanted to cry his name again when he leaned over her and gently kissed her eyes, and from there traced kisses over her face and down over her throat.

Clinging to him, she was vaguely aware of some more of her underclothing being discarded. It was a pleasurable experience. He looked down at her as though to ask, Do you mind? For answer she stretched and undid the buttons of his shirt—and loved him some more when he shrugged out of it.

She feasted her eyes on his chest, and by instinct stroked his chest, letting her fingers play in the dark hair that grew there. She touched his nipples.

'Is it all right?' she asked, and he smiled gently down at her.

'You're perfect,' he breathed, and lowered his head.

For long, wonderful, powerful minutes they kissed. She felt his hands at her breasts and her heart increased its rapid hammering. Then his naked chest was over her bare breast, and her only lucid thought, as exquisite pleasure encompassed her, was to realise that Saul had somehow parted with his trousers and was left with only one undergarment. She was now wearing just her briefs.

Elyss was in a no man's land of wanting when, after

tracing kisses over the swollen globes of her breasts and moulding the hardened peaks with his tongue, Saul let his hands caress down over her tiny waist and stroked and soothed the flat of her belly.

She wanted him, quite desperately, and for all her innocence she had realised by then, perhaps from the increasing urgency of his touch, when his hands moved to her behind and, with his hand cupping her, he pulled her even closer up against him, that Saul quite desperately wanted her too.

Which to her mind made what came next a nonsense: she was his for the taking, but when he placed his hands inside her briefs, and she felt the warm caress of his palms against her naked buttocks, some hidden thread of shyness—which, apart from one isolated moment, had been conspicuous by its absence—chose that moment above all others to make its presence felt.

'Don't!' she protested jerkily, when it seemed Saul was about to remove her briefs and take from her her last remaining scrap of modesty.

He halted—at once, he halted. 'Don't?' he echoed, seeming, at this late stage, not to be believing what he was hearing.

'I'm sorry,' she apologised immediately. 'I'm—er—not very clever at—um—this sort of thing!' She smiled at him then. 'I mean *do*,' she corrected, and because she corrected, and because she realised that if that wasn't blatantly asking him to make love to her she didn't know what was, she flushed a brilliant scarlet.

She almost apologised again. But as she looked up at Saul, and he stared down into her crimson face, so it was just as if he, belatedly too, was taking stock of the situation.

'What the hell do I think I'm doing?' she heard him groan beneath his breath.

She almost teased that if he didn't know, then she didn't either. But all at once he didn't seem in a mood to be teased. She saw him glance down at her naked throbbing breasts, watched as a muscle started to tick a beat in his temple. 'What...?' she began, but didn't get to finish.

In the next moment Saul was wrenching his gaze from her breasts and breaking away from her, reaching for his trousers as he did so. 'Get dressed,' he gritted.

True, she had never been made love to like this before, but she stared at him witlessly. Nothing she had heard had prepared her to believe that this was the way it went.

'Get dressed!' she repeated, feeling stunned. She had been high up there in the land of enchantment—she couldn't so swiftly come down.

'I'm taking you home!' Saul snarled—and it was the aggressiveness in his tone more than anything that got to her.

'Thanks—for nothing!' she spat—and could have groaned to herself. She hadn't meant, Thanks for not making love completely to me—there again, she was unsure what she did mean.

She need not have concerned herself, however, because she had been talking to his departing back as, collecting his shirt and shoes as he went, Saul left her the room to herself.

For the next few minutes, as Elyss got back into her clothes, she wasn't conscious of thinking anything—but was starting to be the most angry she had ever been in her life. She was dressed and ready when, glancing through the window, she saw that Saul—it seemed as if he didn't trust himself to be in the same building with her just then—was standing with his back to her at the rear of the cottage, his hands thrust deep into his pockets and staring out over the fields.

Well, if he was waiting for her, she wouldn't keep him hanging about much longer! Elyss was glad to feel her anger building up inside her. Who the devil did he think he was to take her up to such dizzying heights and then drop her flat?

Oh, and the shame of it—how could she have clung to that uncaring monster the way she had? Uncaring? What else! Her breath caught in a dry sob. Was it the act of someone who cared to play fast and loose with her emotions? And where was her pride? Oh, where was her pride?

Her pride, she discovered as she left the bedroom, was arriving with a vengeance. By the time she had replayed Saul's 'Get dressed' and his snarled 'I'm taking you home' as she went down the stairs, through the door and into the kitchen, her pride was up in arms.

'I'm taking you home'. You've been a naughty girl; I'm taking you home! Rot in hell, Saul Pendleton, she fumed. She had never thought of herself as an impulsive person by nature, but when she spotted the Ferrari keys where Saul had dropped them down on the kitchen table, she learned that, when pushed, when furious, when fury and outraged pride mixed, she could be every bit as impulsive, and more, as the next person.

She had never driven a Ferrari before. But never had she been so incensed before. With her outrage growing by the second, she did not suppose it was vastly different from any other car.

So far as she knew, Saul was still at the back of the building; his car was at the front. Scooping up the keys, she went swiftly and silently to the front door. Just as silently, she let herself out. Making barely a sound, she opened the driver's door of the Ferrari.

She didn't close it again until she'd had a good look at all the controls. Then she turned the key in the ignition, started the engine, slammed the door, moved fast into reverse and—oh, too, too beautiful—had time only to see the utterly flabbergasted expression of Saul as he came hellbent round the corner to see what was happening. Then, his astounded expression one she would cherish for a while, she changed out of reverse, into forward gear, and was away. Put that in your drum and bang it, Pendleton!

Elyss had taken some small solace in leaving Saul— Get dressed—Pendleton stranded. She hoped Saul—I'm taking you home—Pendleton, was stuck in that remote spot until doomsday. She drove a good two miles before she came to anything remotely resembling a main road. She hoped he enjoyed the walk!

Long before Elyss reached his apartment building, though, she had started to hurt. She had no idea why he had done what he had—heartlessly dropped her from those rapturous heights—nor what his idea in taking her to that 'house party' was in the first place.

He had said he wanted to explain. But, given that she hadn't thought him the explaining sort, what was there to say? Possibly there was a reason why he had taken her to the Norfolk cottage to begin with—she guessed she could run for any sort of explanation now. But it certainly hadn't been to take another sample of the kind of lovemaking they'd shared in Greece, that was for sure.

In fact, now that she cooled down, it seemed to her that maybe he *had* intended making love to her. Until she'd accused him of believing her to be some cheap tart who could be bought for a few car repairs. Had she offended him with that remark? Was that why he'd stopped?

She remembered the way he'd tried to silence her with that sharp 'Enough'. Only she wasn't to be silenced—not until he'd kissed her anyway.

Oh, Saul. Those kisses. Oh, Elyss, you chump! Elyss brought herself up short. So what had happened to her taking jolly good care that there wouldn't be any kissing this weekend? Well, she hadn't started it! And what about not by word, look or deed was she going to give away how very much she loved him? Oh, Lord, did pinching his Ferrari from right under his very nose cancel out any signs he might have seen of how she felt about him? Men were territorial about their cars, weren't they? Did the fact that she had snaffled his make everything else pale into insignificance? She fervently hoped so.

If Bernard was surprised to see her again so soon, he hid it very well when she went in, weekend case in hand, to exchange one set of car keys for another. 'Technical hitch,' was the best she could summon up, should he wonder at seeing her again only hours after she'd told him that they were going to stay with friends. She handed Bernard the keys of the Ferrari and asked him to park it. 'Mr Pendleton will be along later,' she smiled, and waited only for Bernard to bring her car round, then she got out of there.

Her parents were surprised to see her when, very late that evening, she arrived at their Devon home. She'd had two choices as she saw it: go back to the flat and suffer the enquiring glances of the flatmates whom she had told she was going away for the weekend, or go and stay in Devon until tomorrow.

'You look tired. What have you been up to?'

Oh, Mother! 'Nothing in particular,' Elyss answered her parent. 'The garden's looking good.'

'It's coming into shape,' her mother replied.

'You're still coming down next weekend?' her father questioned.

'Wouldn't miss your birthday dinner,' Elyss answered, and felt then that she never wanted to go back to London.

Only to get up on Sunday morning feeling restless and wanting to go somewhere, anywhere, feeling that wherever she went that restlessness would go with her.

No one was home when, quite late that evening, she returned to the flat and went to ring her parents. Feeling listless, Elyss rang their number. 'Made it in one piece,' she informed her mother.

'You're all right, dear?' her mother queried. 'Both your father and I thought you were a little bit quiet.'

Oh, heavens, the last thing she wanted was to worry them. 'I'm fine!' she protested. 'Don't worry about me. Life's great,' she enthused. She later went to her room feeling at rock bottom. How great was it to be in love with somebody whom she was unlikely ever to see again? Saul had turned her world upside down and, given she'd pinched his car—had she really done that?—he'd walked away laughing.

See him again she might not—but on Monday, the very next day, when, in low spirits, she returned home from her office, Elyss had very good proof that Saul was not permanently stranded in Norfolk where she had left him.

Proof that he had made it back to London came via a letter waiting for her. Not a letter from him, but a handwritten envelope that had, from the absence of a stamp, been specially delivered.

'How are you?' she questioned Nikki. No one else was home yet. She might have asked if Nikki had seen who had delivered her letter, but Nikki was looking particularly downcast.

'I've had one of my one step-back days,' Nikki answered unhappily, and Elyss paused to sympathise with her—Nikki's progress seemed to be two steps forward, then one step back.

'You're still much better than you were,' Elyss encouraged. 'Give me a minute to change and I'll be out for a chat.'

All thoughts of going back into the sitting room, however, went completely from her mind when, in her bedroom, Elyss slit the envelope and took out a single sheet of paper. It was not a letter, but a bill. A bill from a garage for repairs carried out to one Ferrari car.

She sank down onto the bed, gasping at the amount while at the same time trying to adjust to the fact that she had received the bill at all!

It was a mistake, she realised. The bill should not have come to her. Elyss then raised her eyes to see to whom the bill was addressed. It was addressed to Saul! She checked the envelope, the firm, masculine writing—and suddenly she was furiously angry.

The swine! The diabolical swine. He—Saul Pendleton—had sent her this bill! No note, just the bill. He, when the account had been sent to him—he, when she had thought the account settled—had sent it on to her for payment!

How *could* he? He knew full well that she couldn't pay it! But, in any case, she no longer owed him anything. It was he who had said that after that 'house party'

last weekend her debt would be settled. Just as it was
Saul—rotten, rat-fink Pendleton—who had, on Saturday,
snarled, 'I'm taking you home'—not that she would
have stayed anyway, after his harsh 'Get dressed' when
she'd been up there on Cloud Nine. But it was he who
had foreshortened the weekend, not her—and now this!

Well, he could go whistle! Elyss was so angry she
tore the bill into shreds and tossed it in her wastebasket.
How could he? she fumed again as she changed out of
her smart business two-piece suit.

It just showed how much he cared—though didn't
care seemed to fit better! Surely he couldn't be serious?
Elyss left her room with sweet pictures in her head of
one Saul Pendleton stretched out on some rack with her,
Elyss Harvey, slowly and gleefully turning the handle.

But that hugely satisfying picture went skidding when
reality entered and she caught Nikki watching her. Oh,
Lord, she'd forgotten Nikki—the poor love still wasn't
up to dealing with the likes of Saul Pendleton.

'Is anything the matter, Elyss?' Nikki asked, causing
her to realise that her face must be much more expres-
sive than she had realised.

'No. No, not a thing,' Elyss answered swiftly. Then
smiled, as she added, 'Only I've just remembered a
phone call I—er—forgot to make.'

'I'll put the kettle on,' Nikki volunteered—and as she
went kitchenwards Elyss, pausing only to pick up the
telephone, returned to her room.

She didn't want to ring him, she didn't. If it was left
to her she wouldn't, she wouldn't. Let him sue her for
the money—'I thought, when I went away with him for
the weekend, your honour, that my debt was paid.' That
would look lovely in the papers, wouldn't it, Mr Next
Chairman of Oak International? That would give the

shareholders a tremendous amount of confidence in him, wouldn't it?

She was defeated before she began; Elyss knew that. It would look lovely in the papers for her parents to read too! And what about Nikki? Besides, Elyss sighed, she still loved the hard-headed brute. This, she guessed, was part of her punishment for daring to steal his Ferrari.

She dialled his number, assuming he wouldn't be in. He was. Her legs went weak. 'What's with the bill, Pendleton?' she snapped.

'How nice to hear from you, Elyss,' he answered pleasantly.

She wasn't fooled. 'I'm not paying it!' she stated hotly.

There was a pause. 'Shall I come over to discuss it?' he enquired silkily.

The hound! The absolute hound! He wanted chopping off at the knees! 'You know you can't do that!' she snapped. Grief, Nikki would have a full-blown nervous breakdown on the spot should she chance to open the door and find him on the other side!

'Then I suggest you come here to see me,' Saul drawled, and it sounded more like an order than an invitation when he added, 'I shall be in all evening.'

Elyss drew breath to tell him, politely, that hell would freeze over first, then discovered that he wasn't there on the line. He had terminated the call. Well, goodnight to you too! She wasn't going. She'd be damned if she would!

CHAPTER EIGHT

IT WAS just after seven that evening when Elyss, having changed twice and now wearing a plain salmon-coloured dress that particularly suited her, pulled up outside Saul's apartment block.

Bernard was on duty. She wasn't going to be more than a few minutes, but just in case he needed to move her car she handed him her keys. 'Mr Pendleton is expecting you, Miss Harvey,' Bernard stated—and she was glad he couldn't read her thoughts.

Confident, overbearing... Elyss fumed as she rode up in the lift. Expecting her, was he? Certain she would come, was he? She stepped out of the lift—and abruptly, worryingly, suddenly felt her anger drain away. She wanted it back, needed it back. Wanted to be as angry as she'd been before, when she had first slit that handwritten envelope.

Oh, heck—she didn't want to see him, hadn't wanted to come. But, since it seemed the matter wasn't yet resolved, she had to go on. She wanted it over and done with *now*. This was no time to be cowardly.

Elyss reached his door—and took a few seconds to compose herself—then she rang the doorbell.

It was opened too quickly. If Saul had been standing the other side waiting for her to press the bell, she supposed he couldn't have answered the door more quickly. But she wasn't ready—would never be ready, she realised.

'What kept you?' she snapped, sharp, acid, for openers, guessing she had Bernard to thank that Saul was aware that she'd been on her way up.

She expected some 'lippy shrew'-type remark for her trouble, but even as Saul stood back for her to enter she felt surprise that, while his lips seemed to twitch minutely, as if amused, he had no comment to make.

That alone made her feel nervous. He could be sharp too, if memory served correctly. Oh, Lord, how she loved him, standing there not saying a word but just raking her face with those grey eyes. Oh, how she loved him.

'Come in.' It seemed he had tired of waiting for her to accept his unspoken invitation.

'I'm not stopping.'

'I never supposed that you were,' he replied, and as she crossed over his threshold Elyss was glad to feel a spurt of anger at what she read as a sarcastic remark to the effect that he had merely suggested she come to see him—not stay the night.

He led the way into his drawing room. 'Take a seat,' he invited evenly. She didn't want to take a seat, but she owned to feeling a touch shaky and made for one of his sofas. 'Would you like something to drink?'

A double brandy might go down well. But, since she wasn't used to that particular spirit, she wanted what she had to say to be said unslurred.

'No, thanks.' She was sitting down, so why wasn't he? Mind-reader! Why did he have to come and share her sofa? There was another one over there! Elyss turned in her seat, glad it was a four-seater sofa and he was at the other end of it. 'I believe you have some idea that there is—a matter—outstanding between us,' she charged.

'I couldn't have put it better myself,' Saul agreed calmly.

And that annoyed her for a start—that he should be so calm when just seeing him again had caused her to feel a quivering mass inside. 'So what happened to my agreement to go with you to that "house party"—if you'll pardon the expression—and your subsequent agreement, and I quote, that: "After this, your debt will be settled"?' she questioned tautly.

'Oh, that,' he shrugged. 'That isn't the issue here.'

Witlessly Elyss stared at him. 'Just a minute—did you or did you not send me a bill for the repairs to your car?'

'I had to get you here some way.'

She was speechless. She had thought herself fairly intelligent, but now, she owned, she was lost. She went back to the beginning. He had sent her a bill which she had considered settled. He, only minutes ago, had agreed that there was a matter outstanding. Yet now—as cool as you like—he was saying that the fact of that colossal bill wasn't the issue here, and that he had only sent it to her in order to get her there.

'I see.'

He didn't look too impressed. 'What do you see?'

She was totally perplexed, if the truth be known, but, thus challenged, did her best. 'You're still angry that I—er—borrowed your Ferrari, and, despite that bit about that debt not being the issue, you have every intention that I should find the funds from my almost non-existent resources to pay for—' She broke off when the intensity of his gaze started to get to her.

And owned she was floundering when, his eyes still on her, he said, 'You—if you'll forgive me, Elyss—you see nothing.'

'Oh,' she muttered, in something of a fog. She had

the weirdest sort of impression that Saul seemed a touch
disappointed that she didn't seem able to latch onto what
all this was about. But she couldn't forget the last time
she had seen him before she'd flashed by him in his car,
she had been all but naked. She...

'You're blushing.'

'You're enough to make a beetroot blush,' she
snapped, not thanking him for his observation. 'You, as
well as I, were as near nake—' Oh, grief. 'Forget it!'
she snapped, but rather thought from the gentle smile
that came to Saul's face that he, with that way he had,
had jumped onto her wavelength suddenly, and knew
what she was thinking. 'So what was this matter,
Pendleton, this outstanding matter, that caused you to
want me to come here to see you?'

'You've no idea?'

'I didn't come here to play guessing games! I thought
that account was settled, but...'

'The car, and repairs to it, ceased to be an issue some
while ago.'

Elyss stared at him blankly. Where did he get off,
being so clever? For the life of her she couldn't see what
he was hinting at.

'You're saying that the account for those repairs is
settled? That I owe you nothing?' she questioned slowly.
He nodded, his eyes fixed on her face. She confessed to
being completely bewildered. 'Then, what...?'

'But there is an issue between you and me, Elyss,
that's still outstanding,' Saul stated—and as Elyss experienced a warning roaring in her ears so she knew that
it was time to leave.

'Goodnight and goodbye!' she bade him swiftly, and
without more ado she was on her feet, already starting
to spring across the carpet.

Saul moved fast. She had gone no more than five steps when he caught her. She strove furiously to snatch her arm out of his firm grip, but he would not let her go.

'Running away from a fight, Miss Harvey?' he questioned mildly. 'That isn't like you!'

Watch my heels! 'Look here, *Mister* Pendleton,' she erupted, 'it's obvious you and I have nothing to discuss, and that you were just playing silly devils for your own amusement when you sent that bill on to me, but—'

'There is everything to discuss,' Saul cut into her exploding, panicked speech. She stared at him warily. He held her gaze steadily, and then, as calm as you like, he quietly let fall, 'There's *us* to discuss, Elyss.'

'Oh, no, there isn't!' she shot back at him in furious agitation.

'Shh...' he gentled her, causing her only to panic more wildly when he did no more than catch a hold of her other arm. And, before she was ready for it, he drew her to him and, bending to her, he placed a featherlight kiss on her mouth.

Shaken to her roots by the unexpectedness of his thistledown kiss, Elyss wanted to hit him—and kiss him back. Fearing that she might weakly cling to him, she pushed him angrily away. 'We've done all the kissing we're going to,' she hurled at him, 'so cut that out!'

'You're in love with me, aren't you?' he countered—and she nearly collapsed from the shock of it.

'Shall *I* ring for the men in the white coats, or will you?' she managed sarcastically. And could have murdered him when he laughed.

But was then shaken rigid when, all at once totally serious, he asked, 'Is it any wonder that I love you?'

A numbed sort of feeling washed over her for the first second, and in the next she decided she had no belief in the accuracy of her hearing. He *couldn't* have said what she thought he had just said! But—if he had, then surely it must all be part and parcel of some diabolical game he was playing. A game in which she had no wish to participate.

'You've gone soft in the head,' she derided.

'I rather believe I have,' he agreed. 'And in the heart.'

Oh, help—he looked so sincere! 'Tell me about it!' she jibed—if he thought she'd come down in the last shower, he could jolly well think again.

'I'd very much like that opportunity.'

She stared at him, the shock waves of wanting to believe what he said starting to batter her. She pulled away from him. He let her go and she took a step back, barely aware of speaking or moving as she asked, 'Do you mind if I sit down?'

'A very good idea,' he agreed, and guided her back to the sofa.

Elyss came round from her stunned state to discover that Saul was seated with her, and was sitting much closer to her this time.

She didn't like it. She couldn't breathe; she couldn't think. Had he really said, 'I love you'? Oh, where was her brain? He might have said it but—what utter tosh! Then the brain power she wanted was suddenly there, her thoughts darting painfully everywhere.

Wretched liar! 'How's Madeline these days?' she enquired sweetly—wanting to punch his head. Wriggle out of that!

Saul, to her aggravation, didn't look in the least put out to be so challenged but, sitting half turned and looking her straight in the eye, he murmured, 'Ah! I rather suspected you'd want that clearing up before you'd be prepared to listen to me.'

He was right there. Though from her point of view Elyss was more prepared to go than to stay and listen. Which made it a mystery to her that, when all her instincts were ready for flight, she stayed there to scoff, 'You're not going to try to tell me that your affair with her is over, I trust?'

'Love hurts, doesn't it?' he answered, and while Elyss was thinking in terms of trying a karate chop—somewhere in the middle of his neck—Saul went on, 'No, I'm not going to tell you that.' It was all she needed to hear—that his affair with Madeline was still going on. It was the boost her pride needed to get her out of there.

'Fickle swine!' she accused, and stood up—only to be pulled down again.

'I'm not going to tell you that,' Saul uttered shortly while she was getting her breath back, 'because I was never, at any time, having an affair with her.'

'Tut tut, Mr Pendleton!' Elyss jeered. 'You must think me stupid as well as—'

'I think you're wonderful,' he cut in. 'And if you could manage to shut up for a few minutes, I'll explain...'

'*Don't* you tell me to shut up!' Elyss butted in, affronted. 'And I don't *need* your explanations. I saw with my own eyes the intimate way in which the two of you were together, so...'

'Don't talk rot!'

'Oh, very lover-like!'

He grinned, it seemed he just had to, and, while she was all in favour of making a clay model of him and sticking a plentiful supply of pins in it, he added 'You are, without a doubt, wonderful.'

She looked at him and, when all the odds were against it, she wanted to smile. Well, it wasn't every day that the man she was in love with said he thought her wonderful—and repeated it.

'So explain,' she invited shortly—and weakly in her own opinion—but Saul, it seemed now, had always had the power to make a nonsense of her. 'Not that I'm in any way interested,' she added, with some sense of having let her side down. 'But I've nothing else planned for this evening, and it's a boring night on TV.'

Saul, to her surprise, didn't take offence at her remarks. Indeed, he seemed keen to have the chance to explain, because he wasted no time in getting started, and at once confided: 'To begin with, it was merely an embarrassing irritant that Roland Scott's new wife seemed to have—um—taken an interest in me.'

He had Elyss's full attention. She stared at him, her expression as serious as his. 'You're implying that you were never interested in her?'

'I'm not implying it—I'm stating it!'

Elyss looked into his sincere grey eyes. 'But...' she started to protest, remembering the way, the adoring way Madeline had looked at him, and also Madeline's visit to this very apartment. Elyss swallowed her protest down. Saul might think he was leading her up some garden path, but she would have those incidents ready to slam at him later—let him well and truly hang himself first. 'Go on,' she invited.

'I'm dying to kiss you,' he said softly.

She so nearly repeated Go on, but that wasn't what she meant. 'Try to restrain yourself,' she tossed at him tautly.

'You're a hard woman, Elyss Harvey.'

'I'm no push-over, Saul Pendleton,' she returned, and felt herself go pink in the cheeks. 'I didn't mean...'

'I know what you meant, love,' Saul said gently, and

her backbone melted. He did indeed seem to know what she had meant. He caught hold of one of her hands and, raising it to his lips, he gently kissed it. Then, 'I'm getting side-tracked,' he said, 'and it's all your fault.'

'I knew it would be,' she offered faintly, wishing that her voice was as acid as it had been before.

Saul gave the hand he still held a little squeeze. 'So,' he said, 'let me explain, and get it out of the way so we can...' He hesitated, and then seemed to decide, as if afraid of getting sidetracked again, to get on with those explanations that had to be got out of the way first. 'I spent a good deal of last year out of the country on Oak International business. I'd been in touch with Roland by phone, of course, and was delighted when he told me he was going to end his long years of widowhood—and was getting married again.'

'You didn't know Madeline, then?' If they were on some horticultural pursuit, never mind being led up the garden path, Elyss wanted all her i's dotted and t's crossed for when the time came to hit him with a clump of the plant Love Lies Bleeding.

'I'd never met her. I came home for the wedding and couldn't have been more pleased. Roland was looking ten years younger. It was obvious that he idolised Madeline, and, while some were saying that the difference in their ages was much too great, as far as I was concerned the marriage boded nothing but good.'

Words sprang to her lips to challenge why, then, had he taken it upon himself to betray his friend by having an affair with Roland's bride? Elyss bit the words back—let Saul go on with explaining; she'd have a lot of things which were short and to the point to say later. Though why he should feel it necessary to explain anything to her, or why he would think she would need to listen... Oh, he'd accused her of loving him—said he loved her... But...

Her head was buzzing. 'So—er—when did it start?' she queried, striving to clear her head of her confusion.

'Madeline showing an interest in me?' Saul thought for a moment. 'I can't pinpoint it exactly. She and Roland went off on an extended honeymoon, and by the time they returned I'd decided I'd done my stint overseas and was again based here. They came back, and we met at various functions. Because of the friendship and respect I have for Roland I was friendly to Madeline—but I was staggered when, after about half a dozen meetings, it suddenly dawned on me that she had read more into it than the friendship offered.'

'You—didn't make any—um—overtures at all?'

'I swear it,' Saul answered, his eyes steady on hers. 'I just couldn't believe my extended hand of friendship had been taken so much in the wrong way—though at first it was only a minor embarrassment.'

'It got worse?' Was she a complete fool? She wanted to believe him!

He nodded. 'The special smile, the hand on my arm.' She'd witnessed that herself. 'It could have been innocent,' he added. 'But I was starting to doubt it. Then I found I was having to take avoiding action when, at the end of whatever function we were attending, she would give everyone a peck on the cheek—yet come in close when she got to me.'

'You never encouraged her?'

'Not once—apart from that initial friendliness. Then Madeline found occasions to ring me at my office—and I came close to being extremely blunt with her.'

'But—you decided against it?'

Saul nodded. 'I realised, though, that I couldn't let

things go on this way, that I would have to do something about it or Roland, who is perhaps a bit blinkered where his wife is concerned, could get hurt. Added to that, there was a possibility that Madeline's antics could ruin the very harmonious working relationship I'd had with Roland; who knew what sort of business repercussions there could be?—not to mention the sadness of losing a very fine friend.'

'Good heavens!' Elyss exclaimed. 'And I thought my life was complicated of late.'

Saul gave her hand another squeeze and looked heartened that she seemed now as if she might be prepared to believe him. 'Forgive me for telling you all this,' he apologised. 'It all sounds extremely ungallant, I know. And normally I'd keep what I'm telling you to myself, but it's so important to me that you understand—that you know that there was never anything going on between Madeline and me. Well, not on my part, anyhow,' he assured her.

Elyss's heart which had been playing games all of its own when she'd reached Saul's apartment door, started to misbehave again when he said, 'it's so important to me that you understand'. Did he mean that *she* was important to him? Oh, Saul—she wanted to throw herself into his arms, to be held safe and secure—she just didn't know what to believe any more.

'So—er—what happened?'

'Nothing very much, to start with,' he replied. 'I thought by then that I knew enough about the type of woman Madeline is to realise that she might go crying to Roland and make me the villain, the ogre—saying I'd upset her in some other way—were I to tell her in any blunt manner to get lost.'

'You—er—needed something more subtle than that?' Elyss realised. 'Oh!' she exclaimed.

'Got it?'

'I think so. *That's* why you took me to that party! Not, as I thought, to make some woman jealous or, as I thought later, to cover the affair you were having, but...'

'To show Madeline that I couldn't possibly be interested in her because I was much too involved with someone else. A very beautiful someone else,' he added softly.

Oh, goodness, her heart was leaping about inside her like nobody's business. Desperately Elyss fought for calm, but her voice was all choky, and not at all like her own, when she commented, 'How very convenient for you that because Nikki crashed into your car you found someone you could use.'

'I'd hardly call it convenient to have my car crashed into,' he replied. 'But I'll agree you were very useful when, with that anniversary party looming, I was trying to sort out what to do for the best.'

'You didn't think to take one of your other lady-friends?' Her tone had sharpened. Naturally, his sharp ears had to pick *that* up.

'I love it when you're jealous,' he murmured.

'You're not right in the head!'

He grinned, and kissed her cheek, and, while Elyss sought for breath, 'There were other women I could have asked,' he agreed, 'but, when the idea of taking you came to me, I rather liked the thought of it being more of an uncluttered business arrangement.'

'I owed money to you—you wanted payment.'

'That sort of thing—though there was an outside chance you might enjoy yourself at the same time,' he stated. 'There was the fact, too, that if Madeline didn't get the idea straight away, I might have to call on your services again.'

'And I was hardly likely to consider myself "going steady" with you, as one of your proper women-friends may have done.'

'You catch on quickly. Though I hope you're not implying that the woman I love is improper.'

Grief—didn't he know what he was doing to her heart? 'Cut it out, Pendleton!' she said shortly, albeit huskily.

'You're not ready to give in yet, are you?'

'You were explaining,' she reminded him quickly.

Saul gave her a gentle half-smile, and took up, 'So, there was I, because of the sensitive situation, unable to deal with Madeline in the blunt way I would have preferred, when your flatmate attempted to write off my car—and then claimed to be you.'

'You knew I wasn't Nikki from...?'

'From the moment of that first phone call,' Saul acknowledged. 'Unless there'd been a dramatic change in the timid female I'd sent home after the accident, who'd been shot to pieces, the controlled woman with a beautiful voice who rang me the next morning could not possibly have been that same Elyss Harvey.'

Elyss wondered then how she could have ever imagined for a moment that she could try to deceive him—and get away with it. But—he thought she had a beautiful voice! 'You—um—that's why you invented the accident happening at some traffic lights—' she tried hard to concentrate on other things '—that night when I came to see you?'

'Lamb to the slaughter!' Saul commented softly. 'Your attempt at deception didn't get off the ground. I didn't know what stunt you were trying to pull—it could have been you were going to attempt to make me the guilty party, which was why I decided I'd better take a look at this Elyss Harvey, Mark II.'

'It was a wasted effort thinking you wouldn't know one blonde you'd met only briefly—and in the dark—from another.'

'Oh, Elyss, my treasure,' Saul murmured softly, causing her heart to cavort again. 'Do you think that should ever I have seen those rich and spine-melting blue eyes before—even in what little light there was—I would ever forget them?'

'I—er...' she coughed. Spine-melting! 'I—um—didn't fool you for a minute, did I?'

'Not for a second,' he agreed. 'Though I should have seen at once that I was going to be in deeper trouble when, at our very first meeting, I heard myself ask if your boyfriend had brought you. That alone irritated me—so then I went on to find out if your flatmates were all female.'

'You—didn't want any of them to be male?' Elyss questioned, astonished.

'Can you believe it—even back then I had an aversion to the idea you might have a male flatmate?'

'You—couldn't have been jealous?'

'Of course not,' he growled, but smiled as he added, 'Who said jealousy was your sole right?'

Elyss sensed danger. No way was she going to admit to feeling jealous. 'You were explaining,' she reminded him again.

'I'm going to kiss you and kiss you when all this is out of the way. You know that, don't you?' he threatened—which did absolutely nothing for her thumping heart.

'Depending how I feel, I may let you,' she answered

primly. And when he laughed, she had to join in. Then he leaned towards her, and, as if needing some salve to keep him going, he touched his lips to hers—and she so nearly clung onto him. 'Please explain,' she begged urgently, at that moment not knowing whether to throw herself into his arms or run.

'Oh, love, don't worry. It will be all right,' Saul promised, but, perhaps because he could see how disquieted she looked, he went on quickly, 'So there was I, aware from my enquiries before you arrived that you weren't insured with the company whose name I'd been given.'

'The game was up before it started.'

'The game, my darling, had only *just* started,' Saul contradicted softly. 'After you'd left that night I knew you must be a very kind and caring person because you were prepared to cover for your distraught flatmate.'

'You knew I would be prepared to do more when you needed a—a female companion for that party.' Only when she saw that Saul seemed to be greatly encouraged did it dawn on Elyss that she was starting to sound as if she believed him—as if she believed that he had never wanted, nor had, an affair with Madeline Scott. Elyss took a shaky breath and hoped she wasn't being the biggest idiot of all time, because she knew now what she was doing—she *was* starting to believe him. 'Go on,' she urged huskily.

'It was a week later, after Madeline had again rung me at my office on some pretext of needing advice, that I was wondering who in blue blazes I was going to take to that anniversary party—who wouldn't get the wrong idea if I needed to see her frequently afterwards—when all of a sudden—though not for the first time—I started to think of this beautiful woman I knew who owed me money.'

'You rang me at my office—and—er—ordered me to have dinner with you that night.'

'I rather think I just plain and simply needed to see you,' Saul confessed. 'Strictly speaking, there was no need for me to see you before Saturday.'

'Oh?' Elyss questioned shakily.

He smiled, and gave her hand another squeeze. 'I naturally assured myself that I was only taking you to dinner in order that, should we need to have any sort of lengthy discussion, we could talk over a meal rather than during our working days on the phone, when we were both very busy.'

'B-but,' she dared, 'it was—er—something—er—different?'

'Most definitely! I only took you to that party because I was certain you thought I wasn't interested in you for any reason other than the fact that you were in debt to me. The problem, my dear Elyss, was that I forgot that reason and all too soon started to get interested—in *you*.'

'You—did?' she whispered. 'Wh-when?'

'When did I start to fall in love with you?'

Oh, heavens, if he carried on like this she was going to faint. Feeling incapable of speech, she nodded.

'We were on our way to that party, which, because of the respect for Roland, I couldn't duck. We stopped at some traffic lights—and you handed me a cheque.'

'You'd had my car repaired for me and paid the account.'

'And, when I'd never mentioned that I expected you to repay me, there you were, insisting on beggaring yourself to pay me what you could afford. I believe, my dear,' Saul went on softly, 'that I started to fall in love with you right then and there.'

'Oh, Saul,' Elyss protested shakily.

'It's all right, love. Don't worry about anything.' He ran gentle fingers over her beautiful face. 'I give you my word I'm speaking only the truth.'

How could any man look so sincere and not be? Her insides were a nonsense. Yet, even while she started to believe him, there was something holding her back. Something which she was unsure of and which probably stemmed from it seeming too utterly incredible that Saul should love her as he said he did. That made her strive more than ever to keep a clear head.

'Madeline—at that party—I saw you at the bottom of the stairs. Madeline was looking at you as if the sun rose and set with you—you're saying it wasn't mutual?'

'Believe me, it wasn't,' he stressed. 'I thought, when I looked up and saw you standing there, that you'd real-ised why I was having to be polite to her, and even smile at her since there were other guests milling around. I soon realised you hadn't, of course—and that irritated me no end.'

'You didn't like it?'

'I did not. You just hadn't seen that I'd taken you so Madeline would know my attentions were engaged else-where, but chose to think I would carry on with Roland's wife behind his back.'

'You—er—couldn't have told me the truth?' Elyss questioned, but before he could answer suddenly realised why he hadn't. 'You barely knew me, so had to be cau-tious. And, besides, it wasn't the done thing.'

'Oh, sweetheart, did I tell you I think you're wonder-ful?'

Don't, Saul—I still need my head clear. 'You... She...' Suddenly her brain started to wake up. What on earth had she been dreaming about? 'Madeline was in your flat the next afternoon when I came to retrieve that purse I'd left in your car!' Her voice, sounded sharp, accusing.

'Much though I hate to contradict you—you didn't leave that purse in my car.'

'I didn't?'

'You left it in Roland's home. Madeline said she remembered seeing you with it, and called the next day to return it—to me.'

'Oh,' Elyss muttered, for the moment confused. 'How convenient I left it behind.'

'Not for me, it wasn't,' Saul denied. 'Though since she had called it did give me the chance to begin to tell her how I had previously been pleasant to her because she was Roland's wife but there was no more than that. I must have been saying it all rather too tactfully, because I could tell I wasn't getting through, when the phone started ringing—it was you.'

She recalled how long it had taken him to answer his phone. 'I didn't think you were in.'

'I didn't want to leave my conversation with Madeline just then. I felt it important that I emphasised that I had no interest in an affair. My words, though, seemed to be falling on deaf ears, so I went to my study to take the call—and there you were.'

'I'm sorry I interrupted…'

'A timely interruption. I was able to go back and tell Madeline that my girlfriend had just phoned and was on her way over. I took that purse back to the study and expected Madeline to be on her feet preparing to leave when I got back. But—' He broke off. 'Did you have a date that night, by the way?'

'Did you?'

'I lied.'

'So did I,' Elyss admitted, and had to laugh, and was

kissed. Albeit that her heart was thundering again, she was serious when she pulled back from him. 'You said you expected Madeline to be preparing to leave after you'd told her I was on my way?'

'I think she thought I was bluffing. She seemed a little upset—so she might have been thinking things over while I was out of the room. Anyhow, she asked if she could have tea, and since it seemed churlish to refuse—though I was hoping you'd arrive sooner rather than later—I saw to it she had some. She was still there when you rang the bell. I was very relieved to see you.'

'Poor Saul,' Elyss sympathised, for once glad that she had experience of Nikki and the way she had chased after Dave, and knew that it was possible for women to chase after men they were taken with. She realised that, even had that purse not been carried by Saul's companion, there was every possibility that Madeline would have used it as an excuse to call on Saul.

'Are you going to kiss me?' Saul asked.

'Do you think I should?' she asked, feeling shy suddenly.

'Do you believe me?'

She kissed him. She leaned forward, and kissed him. It was all the answer he wanted. She trusted him, and therefore must believe him. Saul gathered her into his arms.

'I love you so,' he told her as their kiss broke and he looked tenderly down into her trusting blue eyes.

'Oh, Saul,' she whispered tremulously.

'Keep trusting me, my darling,' he breathed, gently kissing her. 'Ask me anything you need to know. If there's anything I've left unsaid... If, before you can tell me of your feelings for me, you need to hear any...'

'I—um...' She wanted to tell him that love him she

did, but she was still trying to convince herself that this really was happening—that Saul had actually told her he loved her. 'I'm all at sixes and sevens,' she confessed. 'Er—I was that particular Sunday as I drove home.'

'You were starting to care?'

'I told myself it was purely the stress of everything that had happened of late.'

'But it wasn't?'

'You—sound—as if you really want to know?'

'Not to labour the point, but I'm desperate to know.'

'That I feel the same?'

'As me? You love me, as I love you?' Saul urged.

Elyss looked at him. Saw anxiety in every taut line of him—and could hold back no longer, her shyness winging away. 'How on earth could I not love you, Mr Pendleton?' she laughed—and the next she knew she was close up against his heart, being kissed, held tightly, and being generally made breathless.

'Oh, how I love you, how I adore you,' Saul breathed into her hair. 'Tell me again.'

'I love you,' she said, and adored him when he traced tiny kisses over her face and throat.

'Forgive me,' he breathed, 'I've been too long away from you.'

'Two days,' she murmured.

'Two long, hard, gut-wrenching, wearying days. Where did you go? I tried to phone—no one was ever in.'

He'd phoned! 'Devon,' she answered.

'It's not your father's birthday, though?' he questioned, a smile in his voice, reminding her that she had used it as an excuse for leaving Greece.

'It's his birthday this coming Saturday,' she answered. 'Saul?'

There was a question there. He kissed her. 'Anything you want to know, just ask. I want no secrets between us, or anything at all to puzzle you. I want everything out in the open.'

It was what she wanted too. 'Why did we go to Greece? To the villa?' she asked. 'I mean, I can understand why you had to go to the anniversary party—because Roland might think it odd if you didn't go—but...'

'Oh, sweet love. To start with I'd no intention of going to the island, even though Roland had more or less insisted that while we were in Greece on business I stay with them. But you were always in my head and, after seeing you that Sunday you called for that purse, I spent a whole week resisting the temptation to phone and ask you out.'

'You thought it better not to see me?'

'My instincts for self-preservation must have been on full alert,' he smiled. 'I didn't know then that I was falling in love, and with no chance of doing anything about it,' Elyss shyly kissed him—and was doubly kissed in return for her impulsive gesture. 'Anyhow,' he continued, after some long moments of just looking and looking at her, 'there was I last Monday, talking to Roland in my office, not wishing to offend him and searching at the same time for some valid-sounding reason why I must decline his invitation to spend some time at his Greek villa. Then, as ever, I thought of you. And there it was, the answer. So I told Roland that I was rather involved with you just then and didn't wish to leave town for longer than I had to. To which he replied, why didn't I bring you along?' Saul kissed her. 'Imagine my surprise when I realised that I rather quite liked the idea of spending some days with you.'

'Did you?' Elyss smiled.

'I was able to reason, of course, that it seemed quite logical because by bringing you along it would show Madeline Scott that there was only one woman I was interested in.'

Elyss was feeling quite enchanted. 'You threatened to summons Nikki if I didn't go with you.'

'I was bluffing.'

'You were…!'

'Bearing in mind her nervous state, I'd never have done anything to make her worse.'

'Oh, I do love you,' Elyss cried, and found she was no longer sitting on the sofa with him but lying down with him. Saul, propped up on one elbow, was looking down at her.

'And I, my most lovely darling, love you,' Saul breathed throatily, and as his head came down he kissed her long and lovingly—and then manfully made an effort to remember what they'd been talking about. 'I only realised how much I had missed seeing you when you turned the corner as I waited in your firm's car park that Monday—suddenly my heart started to rejoice.'

'Oh, how wonderful,' Elyss sighed, growing more and more secure in his love with every word he spoke.

'I don't know about wonderful,' Saul teased. 'A lot of it has been fairly hellish.'

'I've been there,' she acknowledged.

'Oh, darling, I've hurt you.'

'I'm feeling no end better already,' she quickly promised, but couldn't resist asking, 'So what—er—was a bit hellish for you?'

'You, mainly,' he acknowledged. 'We'd barely landed in Greece and you were jibing, "Afraid of getting lost"—and the very next day I knew I *was* getting lost—over you. Lost to all reason.'

'The next day!'

Saul smiled down at her. 'I realised I cared more than a little about you the night before, when I felt pushed to come and assure you, should you have felt in need of any assurance, that you'd be all right while Roland and I were away for the following day.'

'You kissed me,' Elyss recalled dreamily.

'And realised then when I wanted to kiss you again—and to go on kissing you, that it was a fine way to show you you'd come to no harm. I left while I still could—and was hard put to concentrate on the business I left the island to do the next day.'

'You—um—thought about me?'

'Constantly,' Saul replied softly. 'I couldn't wait to get back to you. But didn't know why until, having spotted you from my room going down to the beach in your swimsuit, I thought a swim a marvellous idea.'

'You came after me?' Was this wonderful or was this wonderful! She was enraptured.

'As quickly as I could get changed and come after you.'

'I remember knowing as we swam that I'd never felt happier,' Elyss confessed with a shy smile, realising that, with Saul giving so much, revealing so much of his inner self, it was time she gave too.

'Oh, sweet love,' he breathed. Tenderly he kissed her.

'I think the way I feel now surpasses the happiness I felt then,' Elyss admitted when Saul eventually pulled back, and she basked in the adoring look in his eyes.

'I held you then,' he murmured softly. 'Held you out of the water, and in my arms. I knew why I could barely wait to get back to you.' Almost reverently he placed a light kiss on her brow. 'Then it was, my darling, that I knew I was heart and soul in love with you.'

'You knew then,' she sighed, and vividly remembered the moment—something had seemed to happen to her too. Though it wasn't until later that she had acknowledged what it was. 'We kissed,' she recalled.

'Oh, how we did,' he agreed, 'and it was all so overwhelming.'

'Overwhelming?'

'You got uppity when you spotted we were being observed, and I, with my heart hammering, was so overwhelmed with this newly discovered love I had for you I had to let you go. There were thoughts and feelings going on inside me that I'd never dreamt I'd experience. Also an instant vulnerability, an uncertainty about everything except what you were doing to me. You said, ''Your girlfriend's watching!'' and I was so shaken just then I didn't deny Madeline was my girlfriend, but accepted your accusation for the cover I needed while I attempted to get myself back together again.'

'Oh, Saul.' By some telepathic sensitivity they moved as one to sit up, and remained in each other's arms. 'It—um—sounds as if it was something of a shock to you,' she said softly, exchanging a lingering, heart-racing kiss with the man she loved, the man who loved her.

'Shock—I was rocked!' Saul revealed, relaxing back against the sofa with Elyss safely tucked into his shoulder. 'But, even so, you came first. Knowing you were upset, but not wanting you to be I grabbed your towel from the beach and as soon as I was showered and dressed I came to see you. Er...'

'Don't!' she squeaked, remembering how, stark naked, she had emerged from the bathroom to find him there.

'You're beautiful,' Saul grinned, and she wasn't sure then whether he meant face or body. Even though there was such openness between them now, she found that there were still reserves of shyness in her that prevented her from asking.

'You kissed me,' Elyss said, 'and...'

'And?'

'And I wanted to say, I love you.'

'You did? Then?'

'I didn't think it. It was—just there, and was the reason why I'd been so decidedly out of sorts ever since I'd met you. The unaccustomed jealousy that...'

'I knew it!' Saul sounded delighted. 'Oh, my dear, you've no idea of how I've clung to the belief that I've heard jealousy in your voice, even when you were denying it. All this last weekend I really needed some hope to cling on to.'

'I always have considered you far too clever,' she teased him lovingly. But then she owned, 'Yes, I was jealous, and dreadfully bruised, and all ready to leave Greece when, right in the middle of our—um...'

'Making love?' Saul supplied.

'Loving each other,' Elyss opted, a tinge of hurt still in there somewhere, for all she was growing and growing in confidence that Saul truly loved her, 'you didn't seem to care a button for me when Madeline came calling. You went with her like a shot.'

'Oh, Elyss, Elyss, my little love, do you think I wanted to go? I didn't. But there we were, loving each other, when Madeline's knock at your door shattered our lovemaking. Then you started to panic. So, for you, I did the only thing I could do. I got out of there.'

'For me?'

'Sweetheart, I had an advantage over you in that I could see your kiss-flushed face. Should Madeline have set just one foot inside that door, she would have known at once that we'd been in the throes of love-making.'

'I'd have been dreadfully embarrassed,' Elyss admitted, wonder in her heart at his quick thinking.

'I realised that. Which is why, when Madeline said something about wanting to have a talk, I took her away from your room.'

'Er—may I know what she wanted to talk about?'

'Honestly, my darling, you have nothing to be jealous about! You'd be certain of that if you'd heard our conversation.' Elyss waited. And Saul, after first planting a kiss to the side of her mouth, went on to reveal, 'Madeline started to declare how she was sure I must care a little for her, as she cared for me. But I didn't let it get any further. To be honest, although it was still important that Roland wasn't hurt, it was of paramount importance that nothing spoiled what I was starting to think, and hope, you and I were feeling for each other. I don't just mean that we seem to spark magnificently well together sexually.' He paused. 'You're blushing,' he teased.

'What do you expect? I haven't been out in this—er—um—kind of arena for long.'

'You're incredible,' he breathed, and after kissing her sweet mouth not once but twice, as if he just could not resist, he then continued, 'Anyhow, I stopped Madeline right there, and told her that I was so deeply in love with you that other women had simply ceased to exist on that plane.'

'Oh, Saul! You told her you loved me!'

'And thereby, it seems, said goodbye to any visions I'd had of spending the next few days with you, concentrating on just the two of us. No sooner did Roland state that Madeline was suffering from homesickness—

a new phrase for being peeved—then you remembered your father's birthday. A week early, you've recently informed me.'

'I'm not really wicked,' Elyss laughed.

'Not much!' Saul teased. 'Though the fact that you were lying, and that I was sure you were lying, did cause me to wonder why.'

'You thought it might have something to do with the fact that I'd fallen in love with you?'

'Say that again.'

'I do so love you.'

Minutes ticked by as Saul kissed her, and Elyss clung to him and returned his kisses ardently. Again and again he kissed her. Though only when his right hand had caressed its way to her left breast, and he felt her tremble through the thin cotton of her dress as he teased the hardened peak, did he reluctantly pull himself away.

Firmly, he gripped her waist. 'We must talk,' he said throatily. 'My darling, help me get my sanity back.'

Elyss swallowed. It was a tall order. A fire of desire had flickered into life for her too. 'We—er—have to get everything said,' she agreed huskily. 'So why...' Her voice faded on an emotional note. 'No, not why... *What* was the weekend in Norfolk about?'

Though still not looking as if he had recovered from her ardent response, Saul seemed to have found a little of his former equilibrium. 'There was I, on that last night in Greece, wondering if any of the physical emotions we'd shared in your room had anything to do with your sudden and urgent need to leave. I so badly wanted to go back to your room again to find out more.'

'You decided against it?'

Saul nodded. 'I was quite happy for Roland and Madeline to leave—I would have been far happier to have you to myself on that island. However, since that idea seemed to be a non-starter, and since I was certain you wouldn't come down again once our packing was done, I took myself off for a walk.'

'Did you think of me?' she smiled.

'You were never out of my head—which, I confess, was already all filled with argument and counter-argument. I wanted to come to your room, but my emotions were in torment with the love I felt. You were my first consideration now. What if I did come knocking at your door? Would you recognise that I had a need to talk, or think instead I had returned to pick up where I'd left off in our lovemaking? The mood I thought you were in, you were more likely to sling me out on my ear than to listen to anything I had to say. I decided that perhaps it would be better if I left everything until we were back in England. We'd be together, just you and I, on the drive from the airport to my place. Only…'

'Only Madeline put an end to that by offering me a lift.'

'Deliberately offering you a lift, I felt,' Saul said heavily, which made her smile.

'You were put out?'

'Quietly seething is putting it mildly,' he agreed. 'Which is why I rang my parents.'

'Your parents?' Elyss asked, startled.

'Dorothea and Tudor Pendleton. They have…'

'…have a cottage in Norfolk,' she finished for him with a gasp.

'They like to take a break there sometimes. I told my mother I needed a break myself. She invited me to use the cottage, reminding me that I had a key and saying she'd ring a woman, who lives in the village, and ask her to stock up the fridge with anything she thought I might need.'

'We didn't get to eat there,' Elyss stated.

'We didn't get to so much as take our overnight luggage out of the car, much less unpack, before—to my utter amazement—you were pinching my Ferrari and zooming off!'

'Do I get forgiven for that?' she asked nicely.

'Now you do. Then I was too terrified you were going to kill yourself to forgive you anything. Only when I got back to London and Bernard gave me the car keys, and I knew you had made it safely back, did I start to breathe more easily.'

'I'm sorry,' she apologised prettily.

'So you should be. Never, ever give me a shock like that again. Dear God, I knew you were spirited—but that took—' Saul broke off when Elyss leaned up and contritely kissed him.

'Er—am I being dim if I ask if there was any special reason why you wanted me to spend the weekend in Norfolk with you?' she asked, feeling a tinge pink around the cheeks.

'Oh, what a time you've given me! Sweet innocent, it wasn't at all what you thought. I'd deliberately not returned to your room in Greece for fear you would misunderstand me, yet somehow it just never occurred to me that you'd misread what that stay in Norfolk was all about.'

'I'm sorry.'

He kissed her, accepting her apology happily. 'The mistake was mine. I'd never taken any woman there before. My reason for taking you there was so we should be alone together, to get to know each other with no one else around, to explain about Madeline Scott, to answer any and all questions, to start afresh. I loved you but you weren't worldly—I didn't want to panic you. But, of course, I overlooked one very important fact—you couldn't read into my mind. I wanted time with you, but...'

'I thought the worst,' Elyss murmured regretfully.

'I should have foreseen that—but didn't. I soon did see, and wanted only to calm you, to try to explain how I intended just a quiet weekend together, nothing more.'

'Only I got angry and wouldn't listen.'

'And I kissed you, and before I knew it my desire for you was taking over.'

Oh, she remembered, remembered the bliss, the fire of his passion. Hastily she brought her thoughts away from those magic moments. 'You—um—told me to get dressed, that you were taking me home,' she reminded him.

Saul needed no reminding. 'What else could I do? I was so enraptured by having you warm and responsive in my arms, I was past thinking until it was almost too late. And, by the time I did have a moment's clear thinking, I knew we had to leave without delay.'

'It—we—it wasn't the way you'd planned that the weekend should go?' Elyss suddenly realised.

'No way. The whole purpose of the trip was in the hope of getting something sorted out, a new start, all explanations said—not seduction. Yet there we were, the bags still in the car, in a bedroom, on a bed. While I admit your shy response delighted me—you must care, you must, to be willing to share with me what you had with no other man—and while I wanted you like crazy, ultimately I wanted to make an even bigger commitment than just being your first lover.'

'Oh, Saul,' Elyss cried shakily. He wanted them to be more than lovers!

'Oh, I love you so,' he breathed, and, no barriers now, they tenderly kissed. 'Don't you see my darling? We had to leave that cottage. I held you in my arms and knew then that there was no way the two of us could be alone together under the same roof without my wanting to sleep with you in my arms. In view of what had so spontaneously just happened between us, was happening between us, I had grave doubts about my strength to resist you, come nightfall. Sweet love, my head was a clashing torrent of what instinct craved and what brain power—such as I had just then—rejected. But topping everything was the certainty that the best way to show that I was serious in my respect for you—you'd made me furious by your remark about my seeing you as some cheap tart—was to take you back to London.'

'Oh, my wonderful Saul,' Elyss whispered, and kissed him, and wanted to go on kissing him. But she it was who broke their pain-salving kiss, however. She looked at him, loved him, and her tone was all dreamy when she remembered, 'You didn't take me back—I drove myself.'

'Outrageous woman!' Saul exclaimed lovingly. 'I was in the garden, too scared to come into the house lest you were in need of being comforted and would lose my head again. All the time, I was trying to determine if the way you had been with me could in any way have meant that you love me a little—and then I heard the familiar sound of the Ferrari's engine. I just couldn't believe it!'

'You did look a bit—er—astonished,' she teased.

'That's the understatement of the year,' Saul grinned. 'But later, when I knew you were safely back in London, I calmed down sufficiently to begin to wonder if the fact that you were enraged enough to roar off in my Ferrari meant I had hurt you, because you loved me.'

'Did I say you were clever?'

'You wouldn't have thought so if you'd seen the demented way I was pacing this apartment when I got back. Had I hurt you? Had you been jealous? Why hadn't I explained about Madeline sooner? Had I lost all chance with you? No, I wouldn't have that! Would you ever agree to see me again to give me an opportunity to explain? To hell with it. I'd go and call at your flat.'

'Oh, darling,' she sympathised. 'Did you—you didn't call round at my place?'

'I didn't,' he confirmed, 'for two reasons—although my self-control was all but shot. But, apart from the fact you lived with three others—making the chance of any private conversation unlikely—you'd impressed on me the notion that the flatmate who crashed into my car would have a blue fit if she clapped her eyes on me again. I realised I would have to try all other methods first.'

'Oh, you are kind!' Elyss exclaimed softly. 'You tried to ring, you said?'

'Many times. Although in the end I decided that any woman who was so boilingly angry as to steal a man's car wasn't likely to hang around on the phone overlong to listen to explanations. I—er—decided I had better let you phone me.'

'That's why you sent me that bill!' she gasped.

'As far as I was concerned, the only matter outstanding was the fact that I loved you, and if I hadn't read what signs there were completely wrongly, that you loved me. But how was I ever to find out? I decided not to ring you at your office for the same reason I'd stopped trying to get someone to answer your home phone. Nor, since you could easily have hared off in an opposite direction, was I going to wait for you outside your office. And so, since I didn't intend to wait longer than today to see you, I sent a messenger off to your place with that bill first thing this morning, and left my office early this afternoon, and have been going quietly out of my head while I waited for you to ring.'

Elyss sighed blissfully. 'I'd no idea I'd been such a trouble to you.'

'From day one,' he agreed cheerfully.

'You weren't very happy to have someone make a dent in the Ferrari?'

'"Disgruntled" about covers it. The state the culprit was in! I had to send her home in a taxi. And I was extremely annoyed at the deception when a different Elyss Harvey turned up at my door. But,' Saul went on, taking time out to kiss her lips, 'I found I was so taken with your blue-eyed beauty that I could only thank the phoney Elyss Harvey for crashing into me.'

'Oh, Saul, you say the nicest things.'

'Does that get me an invitation to your father's birthday party?'

Elyss blinked. 'You want to—meet—my father?'

'I think I should, since before too long he's going to be giving you to me in marriage.'

Elyss swallowed, hard. 'Marriage!' she whispered.

'You are going to marry me?' He sounded uncertain. She stared at him. Incredible as it seemed, Saul actually sounded uncertain. 'I love you. You must marry me,' he pressed.

'I'd better—ring my parents and let them know there'll be four for dinner on Saturday,' she accepted tremulously.

A wonderful smile suddenly broke across Saul's strained features. 'Thank you, my darling,' he breathed, and tenderly kissed her.

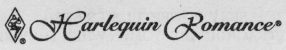

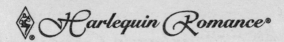
Harlequin Romance®

**Get ready to meet the world's most
eligible bachelors: they're sexy, successful
and, best of all, they're all yours!**

BACHELOR TERRITORY

Look out for these next two books:

**September 1998:
WANTED: A PERFECT WIFE (#3521)
by Barbara McMahon**

**November 1998:
MY GIRL (#3529)
by Lucy Gordon**

*There are two sides to every relationship—
and now it's his turn!*

Available wherever Harlequin books are sold.

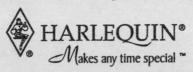
HARLEQUIN®
Makes any time special ™

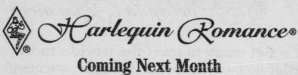

Harlequin Romance®

Coming Next Month

#3527 THE VICAR'S DAUGHTER Betty Neels
It took a tragic accident to bring plain, sensible Margo an offer of marriage from Professor Gijs van Kessel. It was a practical proposal, but, as Margo was taken into the bosom of his family in Holland, she did wonder whether he might, someday, return her love....

#3528 HER MISTLETOE HUSBAND Renee Roszel
Third book in this magical trilogy
Elissa Crosby had assumed a mothering role with her two younger sisters for years. Stubborn and independent, she couldn't confess that her mystery Christmas guest was not the affectionate lover they assumed, but a man who threatened to take away everything she held dear....

Enchanted Brides—*wanted: three dream husbands for three loving sisters.*

#3529 BE MY GIRL! Lucy Gordon
Nick Kenton had a perfectly ordered life—until Katie Deakins came to stay. Instead of the gawky teenager he remembered, Katie was now a stunningly beautiful woman. Worse, she was a beautiful woman intent on turning his life upside down!

Bachelor Territory—*there are two sides to every story...and now it's his turn!*

#3530 WEDDING BELLS Patricia Knoll
Brittnie wished her relationship with Jared Cruz extended beyond that of boss and employee—and involved marriage! At first Jared wasn't interested. But then his grandfather decided to play cupid, and Jared found himself having to think again....

Marriage Ties—*four Kelleher women bound together by family and love.*